TRAITOR
TO
THE
RACE

DARIECK SCOTT

TRAITOR TO THE RACE

A DUTTON BOOK

DUTTON

Published by the Penguin Group
Penguin Books USA Inc., 375 Hudson Street, New York, New York 10014, U.S.A.
Penguin Books Ltd, 27 Wrights Lane, London W8 5TZ, England
Penguin Books Australia Ltd, Ringwood, Victoria, Australia
Penguin Books Canada Ltd, 10 Alcorn Avenue, Toronto, Ontario, Canada M4V 3B2
Penguin Books (N.Z.) Ltd, 182–190 Wairau Road, Auckland 10, New Zealand

Penguin Books Ltd, Registered Offices:
Harmondsworth, Middlesex, England

First published by Dutton, an imprint of Dutton Signet,
a division of Penguin Books USA Inc.
Distributed in Canada by McClelland & Stewart Inc.

First Printing, May, 1995
1 3 5 7 9 10 8 6 4 2

Copyright © Darieck Scott, 1995
All rights reserved

FIC

SCOTT

D

REGISTERED TRADEMARK—MARCA REGISTRADA

LIBRARY OF CONGRESS CATALOGING IN PUBLICATION DATA:

Scott, Daireck.
Traitor to the race / Darieck Scott.
p.   cm.
I.   Title.

PS3569.C6153T7 1995   94-34233
813'.54—dc20   CIP

Printed in the United States of America
Set in Garamond No. 3 and Gill Sans

Designed by Steven N. Stathakis

for Dorothy Scott

My thanks and gratitude to Ian Duncan for being my best reader and encouraging me at the earliest stages of serious fiction writing; to Stephen Liacouras, for his love, insight, and unflagging support; to Ty Blair, Daniel Contreras, and John Roemer for their thoughtful responses to the novel; to Jennifer Fleming, Chanelle Schaffer, Dionne Scott, and Michael Goff for taking the time to read the thing; and to Marian Young for believing in my work.

Junior used to long to play with the black boys. More than anything in the world he wanted to play King of the Mountain and have them push him down the mound of dirt and roll over him. He wanted to feel their hardness pressing on him, smell their wild blackness . . .

—TONI MORRISON, *The Bluest Eye*

PRELUDE: ALL ABOUT HAMMETT

This is how it happened:

Hammett Wade came into the Village most Saturday nights in the summer, wearing a little too much cologne and white pants a little too tight. But that was how he liked it: snug and sexy. The pants went just right with his mauve tank top and its deep cleavage, which barely covered his pectorals. "My negligee," he would tell Warren. Hammett liked the way he swaggered, too. Picked it up when he was in the Army, Fort Benning down south in Georgia, where he learned how to move, how to walk by and casually trail his hand along the smooth curve of his thigh as it rounded into his groin, bulging in those tight whites. How to make those Georgia girls cream. But that wasn't the kind of cream Hammett looked for, and girls weren't what he was after.

"But you just like a man anyway, homes," Warren would say. Warren Hill was straight, a clerk in a Brooklyn police precinct. He went up to the Village on Saturday nights with Hammett and walked up and down Christopher Street, licked ice cream at the stand-up Häagen-Dazs, strolled by packs of boys and men gathered at the bank of the Hudson River on the piers. Sometimes they walked far and late into the night, up to the northern piers where they rarely saw a white face, unless it was fey with a lean wolf's lust, or calm and studied behind round-eye glasses and a small frozen smile. Warren didn't mention his wife on those Saturday nights, unless somebody got a little too close, eyed him a little too lingeringly, or, God forbid, spoke to him. "I'm a married man, and I *don't* play that!" Warren would tell Hammett, and swivel his back toward his admirer's face.

Truth was Warren would say that with his neck moving and a feminine rhythm in his retort that made people think he was about to start flinging his arm and snapping his fingers in the air the way a girl might. Or a snap queen. The swish lay await inside Warren like lycanthropy: if not for what happened, the time would surely have come when on nights of the full moon he would have scurried out to buy women's pink panties in discount stores, and then (with a little careful tucking) luxuriated in the sensation of silk and lace hidden underneath his manly blue police uniform. But Warren claimed to know who he was and said who he was was straight, and so he never failed to walk with Hammett on summer Saturdays, and he knew where all the bars and clubs were better than Hammett did.

Truth was, too, that Hammett's shape had never been that good, not even in the Army, and in his early thirties now that tank top began to curve in a not-too-pretty way just above the belt loops of his white pants, and his chest just wasn't what it once was. What he still had going for him was a deep baritone voice, beautiful to hear—in another lifetime, radio might have been his calling—and thick legs that advertised through those worn white pants. Nice.

But not nice enough, as time went by. Hammett had a little thing for white boys, those with the smooth waved hair, square jaws and cool, cool eyes. He'd had several—his count was up to twenty-two, though in Warren's judgment at least three didn't count. Most of these conquests were marked on Hammett's bedpost after his tour in the Army and before the Plague, in the Park on his knees, or standing and looking down on the head of wavy smooth hair and pushing it, down and down and down again in time with his moans (how urgent, how very urgent and *nasty* it was).

The thing getting in Hammett's way now was his face and his talk, baritone notwithstanding: a row of too many teeth in a banana-long grin; low, short forehead; and ingrown hair bumps all along the side of his jaws. His talk: terrible. They hardly understood him. Women, back when he was straight, sometimes had to hold back their laughter. His language was pitiful—so hesitant, so inadequate. They would ask him to repeat his words, enunciate, loosen up. Nothing worked. His words were pitiful.

And now he was older.

But still he had this little thing for the white boys, who were looking at each other and at swarthy Puerto Rican or Italian ethnic boys, and at black men who fit the proper qualifications. Rarely at Hammett.

All this by way of background: hence, Hammett Wade and Warren Hill were walking back home in disgust that Saturday night.

The streets were not empty; they never were. The two men kept their eyes open and maintained for passersby a faintly lascivious demeanor—wetting their lips, roving up and down with their eyes, that sort of thing. The plan was that if someone liked Warren, he'd reel him in and then introduce him to Hammett, but of the several men who glanced in their direction that night, none was suitable.

At one point Hammett saw a slim dark figure in loose blue short pants and a T-shirt walking ahead of them on the other side of the street. Hammett called out, "Kenny!" The figure, swathed in the shadows of the trees planted along the sidewalk, stopped for a moment. It turned and then held still, irresolute, like a canine lifting its nose to catch the scents on the wind.

"Kenny?" Hammett called again.

The figure walked on, turned the corner and disappeared.

"That your cousin?" Warren asked.

"I don't know."

Warren snorted. "Always was a stuck-up bitch, from what you said."

"Shut up," Hammett said. But his head dropped lower, and his pace slowed.

At length, passing by the piers, they looked beyond the street and saw a circle of moonlight. It rocked softly over the gray water, illusory and precious, like a shimmering blanket of newfallen snow. A tug floated over the light, appearing, for a moment, framed and motionless.

"It remind me of San Francisco," Hammett said, and suddenly he was happy. A friend of his lived in San Francisco, and he'd taken leave and gone out for her wedding while he was still in Fort Benning. Many times he'd told Warren of how much sex he'd had there, starting in the airport bathroom.

Warren merely nodded, being more practical and less impressed by beauty than his friend. But something in the stillness of the picture caught him, too, as he gazed distractedly over the water. He sighed, and for the first time that evening allowed his high, tight shoulders to relax.

Serene now, they walked farther without speaking, heading east. Oblivious, they ambled onto a block where a couple of the streetlights had been broken. Big, squat faceless warehouses stood back from the street, masked by tunnels of planks and pipe built to shelter pedestrians from the construction overhead.

"It's so quiet," Warren whispered.

"Yeah." Hammett smiled. They stopped for a moment to appreciate it.

Then they heard a high, strangled cry.

Abruptly it was muffled. The *mmph,* in the dark silence, they heard like a blindfolded man hears the rifles of his firing squad being cocked.

"Keep walking," Warren whispered again after a moment. "Just walk and don't look nowhere."

But of course Hammett looked.

Didn't mean to, just did.

So fast it happened that he didn't mean to, but did.

Just then, a big car, some kind of Lincoln probably, hurtled out of the silence and swung left onto the street. Hammett and Warren jumped out of the way—Warren to the car's left, Hammett to its right. The headlights flared over the whole street, ignited it in white as the car flashed by, and Hammett, off balance, looked.

So fast: too many to count. Several men standing, eyes

wide, faces red or ashen in the swift-passing light. White pale thick-calved legs of the woman, splayed, kicking at nothing, like the mad, horrible flailing of an insect on its back. And blood, so much red blood along the inside of her thighs, on her heaving abdomen. And the man, the one man standing there in profile, pants bunched at his ankles, bare-chested, his thick red wet penis just beginning to droop.

For a moment—but time was lengthening now; it felt like minutes—Hammett wavered, unbalanced. In the alley the scene went dark. A low growl seemed to issue from out of its maw (he wasn't sure; maybe it was his heart, roaring).

Hammett slammed down one foot and began running.

So fast: so fast he didn't feel his body, just heard wind shrieking through his ears, heard it in his throat. He ran. Oh, how he ran.

Not fast enough. Not fast enough because they caught him. (Had he left the block? Had he gotten even that far?)

His shoulder hit the asphalt and a big pink hand that tasted like urine clamped itself over his mouth. There were sharp pains in his legs and side as they kicked him and dragged him.

In a dank, stinking place they stopped and held him down. His head back aching against the concrete, he arched his neck and looked up. The moon, white and full, shone between the shadowed outlines of two buildings.

And then, against the moon, a heavy shape appeared.

"Let's fuck *him*," the man said.

Warren was nowhere to be seen.

PART ONE

MEANWHILE...

I

GAME

PLAYERS: KENNETH GABRIEL AS THE PROFESSOR
EVAN MARCIALIS AS THE BLOND

Everyone heard it. Once the moment had passed, it was a matter of some speculation among the passersby whether he had been speaking at that volume and in that tone all along, or whether he had suddenly seen fit to announce himself, like one of the insane, mumbling homeless to whom one gave a wide berth. Several persons commented that they had seen the white man before it happened. The black one, all agreed, they had simply missed. But everyone heard him speak:

"In a very short while I shall have to give you a very hard slap. I don't believe I will enjoy it much, but I expect the simple, stinging pain of it will do you a world of good."

They turned to look, peering through the oily shimmer of heat rising from the littered sidewalk, and saw the old man, the dark brown skin of his bald head glistening in the hot sun. They saw him speak without humor or irony, saw his lips and tongue and teeth enunciate every consonant and vowel with sharp precision. His face, with its long nose and fierce eyes behind tortoiseshell glasses, matched the severity of his tone. They thought perhaps he looked like the master of a British boarding school—except, of course, for his color. He wagged a long, bejewelled index finger as he spoke and looked directly ahead into the thick midday pedestrian traffic, scarcely acknowledging the object of his admonishment.

The other one was tall, much taller than the old man. They might have smiled at him, had the circumstances been different: his hair was bright blond, short on the sides of his fashion-magazine face and long at the top, bangs cut to angle over dark, heavy eyebrows. His face was open and handsome, his frame athletic but indolently carried, as if the well-defined muscles of his chest and legs had been placed upon him as a last-minute concession to aesthetic perfection. His skin was taut and smooth like marble, and his pink lips were shockingly feminine. He wore a purple tank top and long-legged shorts, and he walked barefoot.

They were not together, people thought, this unlikely pair. It was a trick of the heat. But then the tall, silent blond turned his cool blue eyes down to the finger-wagging, talking older man, and they saw in the white man's eyes—they blinked, not believing at first—not irritation or surprise, but something like chastened fear. Something like deference.

Around the corner and into an alley the unlikely pair went, the dark bald man pontificating sternly, the muscular youth uncomfortably attentive. Some on the sidewalk paused in stride, wondering.

And then above the traffic's din they heard a crack, like the sound of a tree limb snapping.

Grinning widely, almost crazily, the handsome blond

staggered out from the alley, hands in long pockets, one cheek of his face nearly purple.

The little black man followed closely, gently rubbing the slender fingers of his right hand with the left. He did not smile.

2

KENNETH AND EVAN AT HOME

They stand together before a wide, wall-length mirror framed by an array of lightbulbs which track in bright yellow-white the perspiration on their bodies, stripped to the waist. Kenneth pulls his bald scalp back from his wet forehead and grimaces at the reflection of the tight black curls matted to his skull.

Evan is whipping off his long shorts in a move which mimics their wild and crazy zigzag pattern. "Hoo!" he shouts as the shorts fly across the bathroom floor. "That was great!"

"Yeah. Yeah, it was cool," Kenneth says coolly.

"I mean, there was this intensity between us, better than ever before!"

"Hm. Yeah, I can see that."

"Do you think it was that we were in front of people this time, like playing to an audience?"

"Could be."

Evan gives another exultant shout anyway, and whirls to press his chest against Kenneth's back and wrap him up in a clench from behind. He is taller than Kenneth and his face appears slightly higher than and next to Kenneth's in the mirror. Because of the perspiration, to Kenneth the smell of their closeness—the smell of Evan, at least—is mildly intoxicating.

"You son of a bitch!" Evan says. "I didn't know you were gonna slap me! You went crazy out there!"

Kenneth is watching Evan's forearms, solid and sinewed and lightly furred, crossed around and below Kenneth's shoulders, beneath Kenneth's large, dark nipples. Distractedly he says, "Yeah, I guess I did kind of get into it." Then he looks concerned. "Did I hurt you?"

"No! Not really. But—it was intense!"

They are talking to the mirror as they talk to each other, but for some reason, Kenneth finds that he's uncomfortable with looking directly at the reflection of Evan's eyes. He had never thought he would care if someone's eyes were blue, but sometimes Evan's are so radiant that like the glow of lightbulbs they linger on the retina—this is what Kenneth told him, long ago when they first started dating. Today though, it scares him, almost, that he should have said such a thing.

"You're beautiful," Evan says, and touches his finger to the thin black trail of eyeliner beneath Kenneth's squinted right eye.

Kenneth likes the feel of the patch of rough brownish hair in the center of Evan's chest as it massages, just lightly, the space between Kenneth's shoulder blades. Maybe he likes it too much: the eyes, the hair—he does have a thing for hair—and the arms, and the smell.

"Mm-hmm, beautiful," Kenneth says. "You notice my unparalleled and noteworthy beauty hasn't landed *me* a job."

Evan lets go. Touchy subject. He starts to look for the gray sweatbottoms he must have left somewhere. "That woman who came over to touch my cheek afterward was so *cute,* wasn't she?"

Kenneth's face loses ten years as he wipes the powder off his cheeks with a damp blue terry cloth face towel. "She didn't seem that cute to me. I thought she wanted to lynch me."

Now he's being contrary, Evan thinks.

"I thought they all did," Kenneth adds. He is naked now.

Evan, still searching for his sweatpants, saunters into the living room which is also a bedroom which is also a dining room. "Ken, you will not be unemployed forever," he says, thinking that perhaps he ought to get to the heart of the matter. "I know you know this, and you know you know it, too—how it is for young actors in New York. But think! You'll be totally like *trained* by our Games. And then the right part will come along. If you just let go of the worry. Don't push it. I know it's gonna happen."

"I suppose," Kenneth replies. In fact his unemployment is not, at the moment, the heart of the matter. But since finding out what that heart is could be messy, he says, "You didn't hear about anything that sounded right down at the studio, did you?"

"No, not today. But I'd give you my job if I could." He says this with a snap of the elastic of his underwear against his pale midsection. "Fact, I got a job for you right here." Evan faces the bathroom and mauls his crotch through his underwear.

Kenneth stands at the doorway, arms folded. He looks, to Evan, almost angry.

Evan's hand drops. "What's wrong, Kenneth?"

Kenneth doesn't answer—anger is not a game he likes to play—but here he comes pulling a long T-shirt over his lanky body. He's not exactly smiling and excited the way Evan is, but then he's rarely excited the way Evan is, and at least he's not exactly scowling, either.

"Did you go to the meeting last night?" Evan feels guilty because he has had heavy script duties and has been taping late into the night for the past week. He moves to straighten the sheets on the fold-out couch bed so that he can fold it up into just a couch. He is full of energy and must do these things.

"Yeah," Kenneth answers. "Lots of passion and arguing, as usual. We can't really agree yet on what the next action should be. Some people were talking about a big, wild dance, maybe, in the middle of Times Square or someplace, at rush hour, with like a drag queen brigade for security. Like an orchestrated dance-riot."

"A dance-*riot*? God." Evan rolls his eyes. The couch has appeared and they sit together on it. "This is what happens when people get involved with hyper-intellectual leftist organizations. Bring back apolitical gay men who like to do drugs and go to bathhouses every night, that's what I'd like to see." His eyes unroll and Evan laughs. "Want a drink?" He propels himself into the tiny kitchen that still smells of the fish they fried the night before and begins rummaging through an assortment of fruit juice cartons and seltzer water in the refrigerator.

"I cried today," Kenneth says. His voice floats like a

comic strip thought balloon into the kitchen. Evan looks over the refrigerator door in dread.

But Kenneth is smiling. "I watched your soap. They showed the scene where everyone came to the house to see Corrinne and console her because Ellen's pregnant by the gardener and Josh's plane went down in the Andes. Everyone got so upset and so emotional, and Corrinne started wailing, and I can't stand it when mothers cry, so I actually cried. I haven't even been watching the show and I cried. And that woman is a horrid actress, just like you said. I was crying over this bad actress who has so much mousse in her hair it might as well be a beehive bouffant. Isn't that crazy? A big ol' man like me?" he says with a short laugh.

Evan is beside him now. His speed—he's six feet or more, after all, and with muscles built for looks, not for movement—his speed is unearthly. He places a cold, wet glass into Kenneth's hand, and while Kenneth sips, he asks again, "What's wrong?"

"I don't know. Just . . . irritable, or touchy or something . . ." He could say more. *Last night,* he might begin, *I think I saw* . . . But he shakes this off. His head drops languidly back to rest against the white wall behind the couch. "Anyway, I cried, believe it or not. Bette Davis would hate me. I *like* cheap sentiment."

So Evan reaches over to caress Kenneth beneath his long T-shirt, and Kenneth lunges against him so fiercely that a wave of apple juice splashes the couch.

(For Kenneth this is a somewhat bittersweet surrender, but it won't take long for him to forget the bitter and enjoy the sweet. He yanks Evan's underwear down over the hair on his lower legs and thinks: See? It never fails.)

3

THE STORY OF SWANSEA

KENNETH WATCHES: Today there is nothing. A daub of gray, here and there, peeking through the exhausted blue of the late summer sky; heavy, drooping leaves sated to bursting with chlorophyll—the mulch that is to come. Nothing to inhabit.

Yesterday I inhabited something—a word, an insult, really, a fierce, full-throated "Faggot!" It was a boy who said it. He walked right here, right through my corner of the Park, a cute little girlfriend swaddled under his arm. They were lunching, probably, and the effeminate fellow who whistled at him disturbed their romantic idyll. While the boy gnashed his teeth and spat obscenities, I burrowed my way into his word and curled up, coiled up, cozy and dangerous: I discovered that he was a Midwesterner who used to catch crayfish down by the sewer with a retarded boy whom he was fiercely loyal to but made fun of around the guys on the softball team; that he destroys dorm property when he is drunk and is secretly attracted to Latina women; and that he distrusts the color pink but often dreams that he is wearing it.

Inhabitation. I lucked up on the activity last Christmas when my father gave me a novel and told me that *this* author really knew what was what with today's black men. My father runs a restaurant in Kansas City that boasts the distinction of having "authentic" barbecued ribs to go along with its uncomfortably authentic ambiance—I quote *The Kansas City Star*—and so when he handed me the book I thought: Not the black men I know, baby. But there was a nice bit of musing in it, where the writer apologized for being a writer, because writers are always getting inside other people's heads, violating their shadows, sucking them dry for a few words, for a story. I liked that.

Today I cannot find anything, though.

Unemployment is hell.

"Swansea."

I was looking away and almost missed it, but she said it and now I see her; I see both of them: two women, one middle-agedish, plump, the other younger and slimmer with creamy skin and auburn, shoulder-length tresses. They wear matching passion-red sundresses and white running shoes. The older one said it just as they walked past me. The word was simple and meaningful; it seemed to answer a question, complete a conversation.

This may be it.

Let me play with it a bit, sniff it, swish it around in my mouth before I swallow.

"Swansea," she says. Swansea. Swansea. Swan Z. Swansea is the younger one's name. The older woman spoke in remonstrance, not revelation. Swan Z. That is how the girl who lived down the street from Swansea would pronounce the name—the girl with the froggish eyes and the hair that was always pulled back into a puff-ball like burned cotton candy. "Swan Z," she used to say. "You could be a lady rapper and have a album."

But no; Swansea detested the girl. Swansea. She likes the way her mother says her name, with a more sibilant, lisping *s* that sounds as if it has been plucked from the Spanish. "Swansea's the name of the town I met the man who should've been your daddy in," Swansea's mother says often, and then she talks about the lovely Barbadian sailor she met the weekend she was traveling up to Canada the summer after high school. (Ooh, I think I like this.) "Such a sweet man, with an accent of *culture*," Swansea's mother is often heard to say. "Then Granmama stuck her big nose in my life and I ended up pregnant by *this* prick." Swansea's father, the prick, never responds, has not responded in twenty-four years. He is a big man; when Swansea was little he'd call his "Swani" over to his lap and she'd nestle herself into the soft, sweaty folds of his stomach and move her neck back and forth, around and around, massaging her head against the bone of his sharp, cartoon-villain chin. (Oh, yes. Yes.) Swansea loves both her parents. But they do not love each other. He is white and she is black.

"Your *father* and I are together because a child should have two parents," Swansea's mother told her one late summer afternoon when Swansea was eleven. They were sitting together in the living room wearing matching red taffeta prom dresses (Swansea's mother was very proud of her size four), dipping wet ruby strawberries into confectionery sugar and melting them on their tongues while they watched their favorite soap opera. (But not Evan's soap opera,

ABSOLUTELY NOT Evan's.) "And believe me," she said,
"as soon as we get you through college: divorce. D-I-V-O-
R-C-E. And a plane ticket to Barbados for me with the first
alimony check." Swansea's father did respond to that, but
only to Swansea. Two weeks later while he was teaching her
to shoot a BB gun out in the woods behind the trailer park
down the highway, Swansea told him what his wife had
said. "I'm not paying her any alimony," he rumbled. "Now
aim the gun like I told you."

Oh, Swansea. Swansea, Swansea, Swansea. I am getting
the hang of it; I like it. There's more, too, like once, during
a recess kickball game in the sixth grade, one of the Big
Boys in the class accidentally hit her with the red rubber
ball when he was trying to tag a runner on the other team.
Swansea stormed in from her post at second base and, at the
top of her considerable lungs, insulted him with such feroc-
ity and ingenuity that, startled, he burst into tears and ran
from the playground in high dudgeon and shame. Caught
that right there in the Spanish *s*. Swansea's classmates kept
clear of her after that for a long time, and her reputation
was such that even when she started showing up barefoot in
high school, people did their talking out of earshot and very
far behind her back.

She is of course quite beautiful, in the way of those
mesmerizing mulattas who dazzled a whole generation of
African-American writers—that creamy skin and silky hair,
and her light almond eyes. People, especially boys, would
approach her with high hopes and low desires. While a boy
tried to find sly words to describe the weather, the beauty
of her eyes, and the make of his car, she'd pull a wallet
out of her multicolored bag stitched and woven by Guate-
malan Indians and lay out, proudly, like a new grand-

mother, a long line of plastic-encased portrait snapshots. "Your friends? Relatives?" boy X would say solicitously. "No," Swansea always replied. "These are people I *hate*." Upon closer inspection bewildered boy X would recognize the pictures as selections from the previous year's high school annual; sometimes he might even spy his own smiling face there among the select few, dangling like a shrunken skull around some movie witch doctor's neck. Swansea and her mother laughed about her latest would-be suitors and the monthly revised Hate Parade over chamomile tea and Mississippi mud pie for a whole two years before Swansea's father found out what his daughter was doing and put a stop to it.

Oh, I shall have to burrow deeper, investigate further. Perhaps I'll even skip lunch. I could be here for hours (the new audition listings are not posted at the university drama school until five-thirty—sometimes six). Swansea.

Today I inhabit a name.

4

GAME

PLAYERS: EVAN MARCIALIS AS THE CAPTAIN
KENNETH GABRIEL AS THE WHORE

The captain would have none of it. He passed his blunt, thick finger briskly across the waxed black handlebar mustache beneath his Slavic nose and then tugged at the small goatee on the end of his chin, taking inventory of his facial hair as he often did in moments of consternation. He shook his head, the skin on his forehead knotting. "No, no, no," he drawled, jamming a beaten gray hat onto his head. "No, I don't want nonna that. I just came down here to *relax*!"

The captain strapped a wide leather belt, an empty saber scabbard swinging from its side, around his slim waist. The movement was violent, ostentatiously so, declaring his distance, his strength, his resistance. He harrumphed. "No, sir! Nonna *that*!" But his eyes, unbidden, settled their attention again between the boy's dark, widespread legs.

The captain's lip curled. "I thought you were a *woman*," he whispered fiercely.

"And ah thought you was a *man*."

The reply came from the edge of the bed. The words

had been formed on pouting lips, plushly lacquered red; they traveled out of a long throat and were slow, deep, and hoarse.

The captain heard the words and fought to rebuild what crumbled inside him. His mustache itched. He heard the words and the belt on his waist suddenly drooped; his shoulders slouched inside the gray uniform. It would have been too much to say that he was stirred—but he was.

"Know whut a *real* man does, Cap'n?" There was contempt now. It was too much.

The belt fell to the wooden floor, empty scabbard thudding without ceremony. The gray trousers, spattered with mud, shuffled to his booted ankles, revealing pale white legs. The captain sighed. His knees pressed themselves urgently down and flattened the splinters of the wood planks. The captain's head bowed before the thing between the boy's open legs; his goatee swept over it like the soft, silken thistles of a brush, and caught one near-limpid drop in its trail. The air in the little room was heavy with a hot smell that mingled stench and aroma.

"Now, Cap'n, now," the voice breathed, and there was no pretense of femininity, no pretense at all. "Now, *man.*"

5

EVAN AND KENNETH AT HOME

They stand together in the kitchenette. It is post-scene, post–makeup removal—time, as Kenneth sometimes jokes, for the noncarcinogenic form of cigarette: peanut butter off the knife for Kenneth, ice cream melting in the microwave for Evan.

Evan breaks the silence. "Sooo—what kind of direct action plan has the group decided on? Something like the die-in?"

Kenneth shakes his head. His lips are pressed more tightly together than necessary. "No. Nothing exactly AIDS-related this time. The dance-riot idea seems to be gaining support. I don't know. The action committee just wants to do something that will—" he licks a glob of peanut butter off the butter knife "—strike some kind of symbolic blow against the Republicanfascistpigdogs on the day of the inauguration."

Evan playfully jiggles a bit in front of the microwave,

vibrating the quadriceps of his thick legs, bouncing his shoulders up and down and around. "Hm. And like what sort of meaning should this 'blow' have? Should it show that today's conservatism is like morally bankrupt or evil or stupid or—what message do you guys want?" He opens the microwave door, but then closes it again and resets the timer.

"What does it matter, really?" Kenneth answers flippantly. "The extremity of the act will give it meaning."

"Okay." Evan executes what looks like a dance move and tracks his funny-mirror reflection in the glass of the microwave door. "How about: we could break into all the little condos and uptown walk-ups those eight million blonds who worked on the Republican campaign live in and dip all their heads in mousy-brown brunette dye while they're asleep."

"You say that just to make me happy," Kenneth says.

"Right. Like I'm so into blonds. You know better. I *hate* it that they always cast me as these blond ingenues. I almost wish they'd kill my character on the show."

Kenneth screws the top back onto the peanut butter jar. "Oh, please, Evan. I mean, I know you mean well, but you can't *mean* it, Evan. You can't possibly mean that you hate what you are."

"Why not? You say sometimes that you don't like what you are. Why don't I? Why isn't not liking myself possible for me, too?" The microwave bell rings.

Kenneth vigorously shakes his head and folds his arms. "But there's a major reason why! You know that."

He grips Evan's shoulders. At night when Evan is try- ing to sleep, Kenneth kneads Evan's shoulders with his long, spidery fingers now and again because, he says, he is astonished by the *meat* of them. Evan finds this puzzling. "It's because you are a white male."

Kenneth says this with a bit of sass in his tone, but it doesn't help because Evan starts; he begins to wrench away from Kenneth's grip.

"Now, now! No politically correct police raid here, dearest. Just—!" Kenneth leans close; Evan can smell the peanut butter on his breath and sees that he is at least aroused, but Evan is not sure this is a good thing. "Listen. You *are* a white male. White maleness is the standard. You define what is. What is right is what you are. What is desired is what you want. What is wrong is everything you are not or that prevents you from being and enforcing the standard. Everything you encounter in the world—you can go to *China* and find women getting plastic surgery to round out their eyes!—everything confirms your right to exist, your primacy in your own life. You can't hate yourself without hating the world you live in, without hating everything. And you don't, Evanitch. You are happy. You are a happy man. To your credit, you recognize injustice and it bothers you, but that injustice isn't *inside* you. You *are*. There is no hidden judge within you who doesn't look like you, doesn't have your history—has *contempt* for your history. There's nothing complicating you like that inside. You're all self."

Evan is red-faced. "How can you say that?! How can you? This is what you accuse all the *fascists* of being, all the racists and homophobes and the pigdogs! Not me. I'm *gay*! I'm your *lover.*" He fears that he makes no sense, so he flings open the microwave door and grabs the carton, pulls off its top with a hollow suction pop, and plunges his short, stubby finger into soft butter almond ice cream.

Kenneth's dark hands flutter in dismissal. "I love you. I envy you, hate you, adore you. The whole script."

"You know," Evan says, "you give so much thought to *me* and the *world*. What about *you*? Why are you so perfect?"

"I'm a postmodern intellectual of color. We're neurotic, misunderstood, and living in exile, but one thing we do have going for us is that we are absolutely bright shining perfect."

Evan wants to resist. But as usual in these matters he cannot articulate what he feels must be said. He thinks for a moment, exhales, swallows. "Things aren't perfect for me, you know." He is plaintive.

Kenneth's hands drop. The palms slap his lower thighs. "Of course. Of course I know that."

Silence.

And then Evan, hesitantly at first, moves forward and captures Kenneth's hands in his own and pushes them back behind Kenneth's back, making bows of his slim arms. He can see the smile rising in Kenneth's quietly downcast eyes.

6

THE BOY IN THE BOOKSTORE

KENNETH WATCHES: Rain: there is a squall, and we have been driven away, driven inside, driven from our afternoon walks, our pre-dinner errands, our pining-away-in-the-park unemployment. We dawdle in a bookstore, making the manager nervous as we crowd the narrow, haphazard half-aisles formed by angled shelves and tables covered with books stacked like temples. She, the manager, thinks that something will be stolen because she cannot see everyone. But this is America: people in this country do not steal books. We have only come to find shelter against the squall.

Today I inhabit no one. No name, word, or face called to me in the park; I found no shadow in which to nestle. I sat on the cold bench and balled my hands into fists inside the pockets of my windbreaker against the unseasonable chill and thought too much of myself and my sorrows. (They have become like sore chest muscles after the first day of weightlifting, my sorrows; I like to press them and feel the pain, and remind myself that I have done something.)

So I found no one. And now it's late. Evanitch will be home soon.

There is, I admit, a boy over there, standing at the magazine shelf with his face behind the spread covers of *Rolling Stone.* He wears a loose wool gray coat—too heavy for this weather; he is from a tropical clime and arrived in New York with just one garment for temperatures below 70 degrees—and a blue wool scarf is flung foppishly around his neck and over his right shoulder. I am avoiding him. A minute ago I stood by his side "reading" one of *those* magazines, and caught his eye glancing fearfully from his dark, handsome face over at the muscled torso displayed on the cover. The boy could not take his eyes off the man's brown nipples or the ripples in the man's stomach.

I shifted my weight a bit to let the boy know that I had seen him; I smiled. But he dropped his eyes, turned and moved away. He looked to see if the squall had died, and since it hasn't, he has been sneaking glances at me from across the bookstore when he is sure I'm not looking.

I do not like this boy. He is struggling with his desires. He is running from what he is. He's probably a college student, new to big cities. He has begun to skip classes and to walk the streets with a lowered gaze, affecting absorption in the pavement. Yesterday, I am sure, he went to the museum where they are presenting a festival of the work of an Italian filmmaker. The museum is a block and a half down from a gay porn theater. He wanted so badly to look at the lurid posters in the smudged glass cases (what pictures, he wondered, matched titles like "HUSKY" and "THE BOYS IN THE BACK OF THE BUS"?) that he kept his eyes focused across the street, as if the Korean deli were the most fascinating of tourist attractions.

He came down on the subway, I am sure. He had to switch trains about midway, and he was happy to do it, because he had waited an inordinately long time in the station near his dorm or his apartment. His companions had been thin, evil-looking young black men who, he thought, did not lounge against the wall so much as crouch there, jaguars in the branches of the trees waiting to flash their fangs and bare their claws. And then a man with a high unkempt afro said he had AIDS, asked the boy for money. The boy cringed. I see that cringe in his neck, so tensely bent to the pages of a magazine he is not reading. The boy thought: These men are not my brothers. We share color, but they are not mine. They don't like my coat, my scarf, my penny-loafers.

I do not like this boy. He was not comfortable until he changed trains, and joined a bunch of white men who he knew despised him but who wore clothes not unlike his own. He was angry with himself for his fears and for his comforts, but he eventually let the matter go, blamed it on urban living.

He looks at me again. He wonders whether I am what he thinks I am, and how I came to be. He will only ask this question of me, not of himself. Yesterday he sat in the back of the museum auditorium with this coat and scarf occupying the seats on either side of him and forgot he had no popcorn as he watched the young, dark Italian rake-on-the-make onscreen promise to put the buxom young mother's daughter in his boss's film in exchange for a little nookie. The movie was not really about the rake, of course, but the boy could not take his eyes off of him, off his slim legs, off the unbuttoned buttons on the man's shirt. He cheered the woman's resistance with the rest of the audience, but really he wished that she would succumb. He wanted to savor with her the sweetness of surrender.

I do not like this boy. I will not now look at him; I shall not deign to catch his eye. He angers me. I turn to look at the window. The squall is less in its fury, but continues.

The boy follows my gaze. He closes the *Rolling Stone,* and takes much care and time replacing it on the shelf. *Flesh,* several magazines over and up on the wall rack, teases him; he believes he can see the stomach muscles flexing, believes he can spy at the bottom of the picture a patch of irresistibly threatening darkness. Then he goes, wrenching his head toward the door. He does not look my way.

Today I inhabit no one.

7

THE ADVENTURES OF EVAN MARCIALIS

Kenneth called them *small white men in small homes who work as much as they have to and call it working hard, pay the bills, drink beer, ogle women, love each other beyond death do them part, and fuck (and fuck over) their wives.*

Kenneth has a mean way of cramming a whole life into one flip comment.

Then there're the old guys, one or two of them, old dudes we used to call them, who used to be the small white men Kenneth was sneering at and now are even smaller. They kind of haunt the streetcorners and sidewalks, retired, I guess, maybe widowed. They spook you with hostile looks, but they could have been handsome back then.

This is the old neighborhood where I lived before the divorce, when Daddy moved my brother and me out to the suburbs. The afternoon is beautiful. Light and calm, free. A bright yellow sun that's not a glare but something you can see, a little friendly breeze. I like it like this. Seems like it was always cold and wet here when my brother and me were little.

I came down, walked all the way from the studio on the West Side because it's so nice today, and because they let me off early. Way early. I wonder if I should get worried. Last-minute script changes, Allan said. "The audience response to Vicki is changing everything." Vicki is good, good enough that I don't know why she's bothering with soaps. I watch her and I can't believe it, the work she does in front of that camera. And a presence like out of Kenneth's Bette Davis movies. Watching her sometimes I think I could really be into a woman, like obsessed with her, so much so I'd want to sleep with her, I'd want to possess her. Maybe even be her, and be able to walk and talk with her style. I wonder what Kenneth would think of that if I told him.

The old street's quiet. I can hear birds. We always did have birds. The pigeons made scratching noises at night on the roof above our bedroom. Nicholas used to say they were rats, and they were gonna eat a hole in the roof and leap down on our faces. I hit him to make him shut up, and then we'd wrestle, which was fun. Nicholas's chest had hair on it, and when he got sweaty from the wrestling it smelled different. I don't think I really thought about it then, but it smelled hot. Sexy. When I would turn away from him on my side and beat off later, sometimes I pictured his chest rubbing hard up and down and across the nipples of some girl (girls I didn't know, girls with long hair and no faces; I never put a girl I knew in there) as he pounded into her and she moaned at him for more.

It's so strange, and stupid, the way you think about sex when you're young and dumb, and what you put together in your mind, like wrestling and a smell and even the danger of rats, and how that, the memory of it or image of it, ends up being what you find sexy, ends up an aphrodisiac.

My old street is quiet and filthy. I'm walking slow when I should be going fast. I should get home and read my lines, prepare. I want to give a good performance. I could take my inspiration from Vicki. It might save my job. That would suck. Both Kenneth and me out of work. Kenneth'd probably laugh. He pisses me off when he's mean like that.

"We'll air your next segment with Evelyn on Wednesday, so be ready Friday, latest."

Allan lies a lot. Or he's just sneaky. But I shouldn't worry. They won't get rid of me on a Wednesday. No one dies or leaves on Wednesday.

I hear a ball smacking against pavement. Across the street on the asphalt fenced-in court some high school kids are going one on one. Nice bodies. Did I used to look like that?

"They don play basketball like we did, do they, Marcialis?"

I turn around, and before I even see him I'm already kind of happy and scared at once. I wondered if I'd run into Russ. His family's still here, like a lot of other families. I haven't talked to him for about three years, but I still hear about him every once in a while.

He looks big, meatier. We shake hands and I'm tempted to ruffle my hand in his red hair, but I don't.

"I seen ya on the TV," he says. He grins a lot and doesn't seem at all awkward.

I make my usual businesslike acknowledgment of his acknowledgment. ("It comes across as arrogant, Evanitch, not humble," Kenneth says.)

His skin crinkles around his eyes. He looks older, too. But he's good-looking. I think of how awkward he was when we played the black guys from the other block every Sunday.

"So. You're a big TV star now, huh?"

"Oh, not that big," I say. Lame. "Not *even* big." And suddenly I feel like I might be blushing, like I'm cruising him and I'm embarrassed because he caught me.

He's looking at me, hard. I try to look at his face but see his chest, which is big now, tough-looking. I'm embarrassed, but I can't stop.

"So what brings ya down this way?" His breath smells like beer. I wonder what he's doing at home in the middle of the day, and it's scary thinking of it, like already he's one of the old spooky dudes rambling the streets.

"You live on Upper West these days?" he asks.

How does he know that? "How did you know that?" I don't sound right when I say it. Too suspicious.

"Aah, word gets around, Marcialis. You'd be surprised how much word gets around."

We're both quiet. He's leaving me to twist. He knows I feel guilty. "I don know." I laugh. "I was just walkin around, you know. It's a nice day. I guess my feet just took me back to what they used to know."

His eyebrows pop up. I don't remember him doing that before. It's the kind of thing Kenneth would notice and wonder about. "Hey. No place like home, right? Always good to get home. After a long time away."

I nod, really starting to feel like I want to leave and feeling bad about it. "Aaah! Nothin much here for ya these days no way," he says. I nod. "Hey. Wanna play a round? Show those little guys somethin?"

This terrifies me. "No. I—gotta go. Late lunch. Time to get back." And then: "Sorry."

He just looks at me, not moving. I open my mouth to repeat my lie, then he says, "Ya know, I seen ya brother just last week."

"Really?" I say. Nicholas didn't mention he was coming into the city.

"Yeah. He and his wife are thinkin about buying and renovatin one of the places here. It would be nice to have him back. Bring some excitement back, ya know. It's borin here these days. When Mama dies, I'm movin." He pauses now, and I have to break away from him. Then, "Mister Swish died, that's why a place opened up. You remember Mister Swish, right? The new landlord, fuckin Arabs or somethin, they're kickin his boyfriend out." And he shrugs and gives a little laugh.

I know a dig when I hear one. I'm probably turning red. While we stand there, the basketball smacks the pavement, with that uncomfortable loud pin-drop sound of tight rubber against concrete. In that sound I go back to other digs. I hear them. On the basketball court: "Why don't you fuckin look, Evan?! Whattaya, in *love* with him or something?!" "Yeah, you can suck his dick *after* the game!" And that stupid, childish name, Mister Swish.

I don't say anything.

He shrugs. Big shoulders, too, bigger than I remember. "Well," he says, and now he stares down at me from two inches above like he's staring down at a child. What the hell is going on? "How's yer roommate?"

Got me. It's like when we were kids, the way I felt then: different and ashamed. But just like when we were kids, he's not going to see it. I just glaze my eyes over and don't speak. If he knows, everybody might know, and how am I going to get a job in prime time or film if even the fans know? But don't get crazy. That's stupid. Never happen.

"He ain't—" he can't stop his teeth from showing now in a smile, the bastard "—*black,* is he?"

I freeze. It catches in my throat. For some reason I actually answer. "Yeah," I say.

"Hmmm." I'm so much more frightened than angry. That bothers me. He looks over his shoulder and then looks back, and suddenly his hand is on my shoulder. And his voice is incredibly soft: "Well. I always knew it, Evan. Sort of. You know? I mean, it's okay with me." His hand drops from my shoulder quickly.

And then he grins, and his hand flies back up and makes me flinch before he smacks me on the arm twice. "Hell, after I turned eighteen I used ta sneak out and do the black whores in Times Square myself. Just for a little while, ya know. . . ."

While he's smiling—wide, happy, like he used to—I notice how calm I am. I'm so calm. I know what he's saying, and I know what Kenneth would think he's saying, and how Kenneth would want me to answer.

But instead I find myself hugging him. Was it him who pulled me into the hug? I don't know. I'm hugging him, and he's hugging back, and then I get the hell out of there.

Walking away, faster than probably looks right, I'm thinking about Kenneth, but the weird thing is I'm thinking about Tolkien, too, who Kenneth doesn't really like but I love. I'm thinking about that scene in Lothlorien, when Frodo offers Galadriel the One Ring of Power, the Dark Lord's Ring, which gives absolute power and corrupts absolutely. "Wise the Lady Galadriel may be," she says, "yet here she has met her match in courtesy. Gently are you revenged for my testing of your heart at our first meeting."

Small white men in small homes who fuck (and fuck over) their wives.

Gently am I revenged.

But did I take the Ring, or refuse it?

8

GAME

PLAYERS: EVAN MARCIALIS AS THE SUN-GOD
KENNETH GABRIEL AS THE NYMPH

It was a damp, hot night, a night where a faint mist clung
to the leaves of green trees and made ghostly spirals of the
light beams flowing softly down from the streetlamps. It
was a still night, not dark or stormy but quiet, waiting, a
night of small marvels, where children and gods stood in
awe of things that had no meaning.

If you had been there you, too, might have seen
it, heard it: there, among the slim, shadowed stalks of
the elms.

One, a deep bass laughter and heavy breaths in syn-
chrony with the thud of strong feet against the damp earth.
The other, a rustle in the grass, as of a light breeze, and
shallow, quick breaths, like whimpers to the ear.

It was Apollo, his yellow curls flying. The pursued was
a nymph—an Oread? a Dryad, perhaps?—some lithe virgin
forest spirit. Likely she had bathed in a cool, clear pond beneath the waning moon just before dawn that morning; she
washed herself, caressed her smooth brown arms and her

young face with the leaves of aromatic plants, and then knelt between the roots of some great tree, offering her humble devotions to Artemis and Selene.

Then, poor thing, she lay out on the grass of the clearing to dry in the warmth of the rising sun. Innocent, young, how could she know how exquisite she was? How could she know how he would see her as he rode his blazing chariot into the morn?

And now he would have her. She would not elude him for long. The sun touches all things on the surface of the earth. And touch her he would. He chuckled during the chase.

There! You would have heard her sharp cry, seen the shadows rock, then meld, fall swaying to the ground (that devil Apollo; so suave).

"Now, now, my pretty," his hot breath formed words in her ear, his muscled torso pressed down, stilling her struggle, his hand reached home, where, he chuckled again, all of his members would come to rest by night's end, one way or another. "Heh, heh."

You would have leaned closer then, prurient being that you are, and squinted, puzzled, for you would have heard something odd, something not quite right. Apollo's great golden head jerked up, his perfect body recoiled strangely, like a bowstring once the arrow has been shot. He screamed.

Already?

But, no, his shadow leapt up, bolted away; he was still screaming.

And chasing him, fast and furious upon his sandaled heels, a horror you could not have seen, snarling, slavering in the darkness; a great, hulking, hairy thing long of snout and clawed of foot. It howled.

You would have looked away now, disgusted, for Apollo, poor thing, suave fellow, stumbled (upon a root? a blade of grass? tunic too tight?), and the beast was upon him, threw the god down upon his perfumed hands and soft-skinned knees, mounted him from behind, and . . .

Well.

It was a hot, ugly, bestial thing that went on out there.

Those nymphs, boy, the children and gods said in the voices peculiar to them. They're tough.

9

KENNETH AND EVAN IN THE PARK

They lie together, exhausted, Kenneth's wet body collapsed upon Evan's, the grass itching their bare legs, and no one says anything until Evan sighs.

"Wow. That was . . . *hot.*"

"Mm-hm," Kenneth agrees.

"I thought . . . for a while there," Evan smiles, "that you were gonna . . . really stick it in."

"No," Kenneth says. "It wouldn't be safe."

"You know, I was thinking—when I thought you were really gonna do it . . ."

"Mm-hm?"

Evan turns his head aside, so that he speaks away from Kenneth's face, which looms above him. "This sounds bad, but . . . This evening, when I was coming back from work, I had my Walkman on, and I was flipping through the stations, so I caught the end of this news report . . ."

"Yes?" Kenneth is never particularly patient when it comes to Evan's halting way with embarrassment.

"Well," Evan says, his voice dropping as if to conspire in a crime, "there was this guy who was found raped and killed, here in Manhattan. I didn't get any more details, because they didn't say much more, but I thought, it's so weird, the idea of a *guy* getting *raped,* you know? Even when they talk about it happening in prison. And it just—I mean, not the killing part—but the rape thing—I do have this kind of fantasy about it. You know? About, like, having some gang of guys, like motorcycle guys or rough, criminal kind of guys, but cute, just pull me off the street and grope and fuck me in the bushes, or something." He looks at Kenneth. "Does that sound weird?"

Kenneth shrugs. "No! What gay man doesn't have that fantasy?" And yet there is something about the matter that discomfits him. He had meant to say more, to share something of his own, perhaps, but now finds he cannot say it, cannot be sure, even, what precisely he had intended to say. Evan feels him frown. They fall silent.

Evan begins to listen to the sound of his sighs and Kenneth's. Sometimes they mingle like a chorale, with Evan beginning to exhale just as Kenneth finishes, or the other way around. Sometimes they are completely apart, out of step. Evan becomes lazily enthralled by this.

But presently he begins to imagine that the grass has become bugs, and squirms. Kenneth tumbles off of him and flops over onto his back.

"Look!" Evan whispers, pointing into the distance. "A rat!"

Kenneth's head and shoulders rise, then fall back. "There are always rats here. I had a little picnic once, on

the other side of the Park. It was broad daylight and
swamp-muggy hot, and I had everything set up nicely: barbecued chicken from the deli, and chocolate chip cookies,
and wine coolers and *Vanity Fair.* Laid out on the blanket,
arranged my little pillow, leaned back—and there was this
trio of rats sitting at the base of a tree fifteen or twenty feet
off, just hanging out."

"They were just sitting there?" Evan suddenly feels
good tonight, like a little boy again telling ghost stories
and rocking in the swings on the playground after dark.

"Yeah, they sat for a while, ran around, disappeared,
came back. I couldn't believe it, how nonchalant they were,
just like guys hanging around on the corner."

"Rats freak me out," Evan says quietly.

He squirms again. "Did I tell you I had some time off
from work today and I went back to my old neighborhood?" He says this with involuntary caution.

"Oh, God," Kenneth moans. To Evan, his tone captures perfectly the expression of eyes rolling in contempt.
But then Kenneth seems to catch himself. "Well"—he, too,
is cautious—"anything interesting happen?"

"No. No, nothing *happened.*" But he cannot, now, find
it in himself to be testy. "I just ran into an old acquaintance. I'd lost track of him. But he told me Nicholas is
planning to buy one of the townhouses."

"Um," Kenneth grunts. "Good. That at least will
improve the quality of the neighborhood."

As he speaks, Kenneth threads his right leg beneath
Evan's left thigh and coils it back over Evan's knee. He rubs
between Evan's legs.

"So would you ever think about moving back there to
your old neighborhood, fixing it up?" Kenneth asks softly.

"Mmmm, maybe," Evan muses. He wiggles his pelvis. "But only if you would go with me."

Kenneth snickers; this, Evan knows, is the embarrassed way he receives tenderness.

"I love you, my Evanitch."

He is so sweet, so inexpressibly sweet, there in the darkness where Evan cannot see his face. "I love you, too, Kenneth."

Evan pulls himself up—there is no effort in the movement; he feels himself glide—and brings his mouth down toward Kenneth's. He stops before they kiss, laughing.

"What?"

Evan shakes his head, still laughing, and collapses over Kenneth's slim, tight torso. "I was just thinking—this isn't even funny, it's almost sad—that in the old days I could feel like this, happy and contented and with you, and it would make me horny all over again, like back at school, you know, we'd do it before we went to the library and then go in the stacks and do it again. And my mind is actually saying to me, Evan, you want more. But my body won't budge. I guess I'm getting old." He laughs again.

"Twenty-seven is ancient," Kenneth says. "Well, there's one thing that's almost as good as sex."

Evan smiles. "A Game? But we just played one."

"This one's not—physically strenuous. Trust me." Evan feels Kenneth's face turn toward him, feels warm breath in his ear. "Game?"

The corners of Evan's mouth twitch, but he decides that he is ready for anything. He rolls off of Kenneth and says, "Sure. Go ahead."

Kenneth entwines his lower right hand with Evan's left and laces his fingers through his lover's. They are twisted around one another like snakes. Kenneth is silent. Evan, distracted, strains to hear the rats, but can detect nothing. Finally Kenneth speaks:

"This won't be fair, because I've already prepared. But here goes. . . . Picture seabirds. A few seabirds floating by above. I can see their smooth, white feathered bellies and unflapping wings, and they sail past so slowly and look so bright and perfect it's like I'm on Ecstasy. There's warm white sand beneath my rump, pebbles of it between my wet toes and stuck to my fingernails. There is a cool, soft wind. And a sea, sparkling green and silver, which tumbles into white waves as it meets the sand, and is divided by fields of red kelp floating just beyond the reaches of the surf. But I am not moved. Beaches never move me. Too much reclining, too much silence. You, growing tan, sleep nearby, sprawled over a towel. I reach out to awaken you, but then feel guilty because I realize I have nothing to say. So I look out: there, amid a kelp field in the distance, two dark figures clinging, it would appear, to something that could be the white bone of a whale, or a surfboard. At first I take them to be body-surfers, strayed from the waves, but upon second look, seeing a flock of gulls wheeling and swooping about them, I have a strange, excited chill. Sea carrion, perhaps? Strewn over the white sand at the tideline are swirls and clumps of umber-colored kelp, like the trail of some huge, magnificent sea beast."

"Oh . . . I like that," Evan says after a moment. He had to be sure it was over. "Where does it happen?"

Kenneth shrugs. "Northern California coast somewhere, maybe. Your turn."

"But—what do I do? Just like make up a story . . . ?"

"Not exactly," Kenneth says. He is patient like a

schoolmaster. "Just take some fantasy of us, some romantic fantasy you might have once had, maybe not even about *us* necessarily, and then play it out a little. Maybe even like what you were telling me about—the motorcycle guys. Flesh it out the way it might happen if it really happened."

Evan has long since learned not to be puzzled by these things. He begins to make thinking noises.

"Ummm, okay, let's see. How about this. Picture Central Park, on a clear-sky summer July night. Throughout the Park we can hear reggae music. And everywhere, in every clearing under every tree, there are young, beautiful bodies moving and gyrating to the music. Most are boys, young men, and they're sweating and laughing and rubbing up against each other. Boys of all colors."

He begins to sing. *"Peace has come to Zimbabwe . . . That was right on the one . . . Now's the time for celebration, cause we've only just begun . . . We'll be jammin until the break of dawn . . ."* I'm tired of dancing, and so I'm standing, watching one group of dancers. My hands are in my pockets and I feel high. You're a few feet away, leaning up against a tree with your arms folded. But you're smiling. The music gets slow, with deeper rhythms, and everybody starts to really grind on each other. Then I look at you, you look at me, and it's not even a shock. There's no hesitation, no embarrassment, no posturing. We don't know each other's names, but we slow dance—we're way behind the beat—and I'm mashing my crotch into yours and we can both feel each other in that semi-hard state. You're breathing in my ear. Then you lead me away from the crowd and out of the Park. We don't say anything, just walk down streets, and we stare up at the sky. I notice that I never see the tops of the buildings when I'm walking somewhere. We get ice cream cones someplace—yours is peanut butter, mine's butter almond, but we both know it's about the *cones,* right, and how they're ultimately just phallic symbols—and we find a secluded playground. We drift back and forth in the swings, without speaking, staring at each other, until dawn."

"That's very *good,* Evanitch." Kenneth is pleased. "I like the 'drift,' and the phallic symbol stuff, which is cute. And I love that Stevie Wonder song. Did you just make that up now, or had you thought of it before? Or has it happened with someone?"

"No fair peeking."

"Which means I don't get an answer."

"Which means you don't get an answer."

"You learn very fast, blond boy. But you inspire me. See what you think of this one:

"Picture Rome, in some nameless piazza on a bitingly chilly New Year's Eve. We're bundled up in long, stylish wool winter coats. All around us is the smell of rich colognes and fine perfumes, the sight of dazzling dark-haired beauties, men and women, against the backdrop of a lighted fountain where bubbles of frothy white water stream out of the greenish mouth of a bronze seahorse. (Some god is on its back, probably, but I like Venus, so we'll say it's Venus.) The cafes surrounding us are packed, and three or four languages are being spoken. The stones on the ancient buildings on all four sides glow yellow because there are bright lamps everywhere above our heads. We are being filmed, and we're all extras. People are thrilled and excited. More than once a woman behind us gooses your little butt through your coat—no, say you have on a leather jacket, purchased in Milan; I have on the coat—she's goosing you and I'm getting jealous. When the clock strikes midnight, the director yells and everyone in the piazza, in unison, raises a crystal champagne glass in the air. We all toast and shout. Folks who have them throw up their hats. We drink like fiends. In all the shoving and hoopla—and because that woman's still giving you the eye—I pour champagne all over your head, and then have the gall to lick it off your lips.

"Later, we walk back to our hotel on the other side of Rome because we spent all our money on alcohol and can't pay for a cab. You suggest that since it's past five A.M. we stay up and go to Mass at St. Peter's, to which I agree. But we fall asleep spoon fashion on your bed (it's a twin; we were too embarrassed to ask for one full-size bed). Our clothes are still on. In the late morning when we get up, it's overcast outside. I have a crick in my neck, and your feet hurt. . . ."

Evan waits again, quiet. "Wow," he says finally. Lying on his back it seems to him that they have come to the darkest part of the night. When neither of them speaks, he can only hear crickets. "I like that one better than mine."

"I added that last part for you, to match the swings."

"That was nice. Of course I like the champagne part." He tickles Kenneth's palm with his index finger. "Do you have any more? I can't think of anything. The Rome stuff made me think of something like bicycling in Egypt, and red dust kicking up behind the wheels, to go along with your yellow stones. But that would have been cheating, anyway; Vicki was talking about her trip to Egypt with her boyfriend last week. I wouldn't know where else to go with it, anyway."

"Well, then, I have just one more little fragment. I was thinking about it today. Picture JFK, in the international terminal. You're not where I can see you, but there's a Turkish family sitting dourly in all the seats of the row except ours. (Turkish because of Egypt, naturally.) They depress me because I think they're being deported or going back for a funeral. So I pull out a postcard with a Van Der Zee photograph on it that I bought after some Wednesday afternoon visit to a museum exhibit. Hastily I scribble the half-remembered lines of a poem—something about youthful passion, jasmine skin and the forgotten color of once-mesmeric eyes. I sign, 'Yours, Kenneth,' and bite my teeth so I won't cry. And then just as I see you come out of the bathroom I dash down the poet's name, too, and stuff it into a pocket of your worn-out maroon backpack. When I watch the plane lift off, I don't cry at all. But later in the week I go back to the museum, looking for the same postcard."

"Hmmm . . . that one's even better. Kind of disturbing, though. Is this what you think about when you go the Park? Is this inhabiting?"

Kenneth's hand loosens in Evan's, and he begins to rearrange himself. "Sort of. Not quite," he says. "But I must say, you've gotten very good at this stuff."

"Thanks," Evan murmurs. He feels proud and a bit bashful. He rubs his stomach underneath his shirt. This is something his father used to do which made his mother angry, but when Evan does it Kenneth sometimes is aroused. Though he feels tired and spent, there is still something in Evan that wants to seduce Kenneth—something, in fact, that is always interested in seducing Kenneth.

But instead he asks, "When you had that picnic— when you saw all the rats—was that one of the inhabiting times, was that recent?"

"No . . ." Now it is Kenneth who seems to be drifting.
"That was an earlier time. Before I met you."

"Oh." Evan knows when to give up. "So, what'd you
do today? Find out about any auditions?"

"Uh, yeah. Something. I'll have to check it out,
though." Kenneth's tone imposes a silence. But his hand in
Evan's is still warm. "Evanitch."

"Yes?"

"I was mad at you before."

"When?"

"The other night when we were talking about blonds
and all that."

"Do you know why?"

"I'm not really sure. I felt compelled to be. I mean, on
one level I *felt* angry, but on another—you know how that
is; when some part of you is completely removed and un-
emotional, just kind of critiquing and watching—on that
level it seemed that I was feeling the way I was supposed to
feel. You know? I was feeling an emotion that had been laid
out for me."

"It was laid out for you to be mad? By who? For what
reason?"

"I don't think there is a *who,* and I guess I don't
know why."

Evan will not let go of Kenneth's hand. "Well . . . I
don't understand. But it's okay. I'm not—hurt or anything."

"Of course not. Of course not . . ." Kenneth trails off.

"It really is okay."

"I know." Kenneth's hand grips tighter.

INTERLUDE: KENNETH IN THE VILLAGE

For a Waldorf salad, one needs apples (Kenneth prefers green), walnuts, raisins, and celery (the recipe Evan gave him over the phone—he calls him at work for the silliest reasons—requires only two ribs, but Kenneth has purchased an entire stalk because that's how they're sold). The mayonnaise is at home in the refrigerator. Kenneth eyes with distaste the dully-colored items in the twisted-neck plastic bags at the bottom of his carry-cart. Unlike his father, he does not like to grocery shop, and he hates to cook—especially when Evanitch will not be home to do most of the work. To enliven things, Kenneth tips a *TV Guide* down from the rack and onto a bag of walnuts.

"Oh, look, child. They killed another one."

It is the West Indian woman behind him, drawling (to his mind) inappropriate syllables. Kenneth has made a point

of ignoring her, because she said hello to him in aisle five
(he couldn't find the raisins). Jamaicans, Barbadians, Trini-
dadians, and those who hail from points in between greet
Kenneth because he is dark and does not "look American"—this is what he is told—but they lose interest when
he reluctantly informs them that his home is Kansas City
and he is aware of no familial connection to any Caribbean
island. After several such encounters he has learned to feel
instantly ashamed in the presence of West Indians. He does
not glance over his shoulder, then, when she says:

"Lord, left him all beat up . . . an, oooh, *sodomized*.
Lord."

Her hand enters his peripheral vision, a long, discolored, indented scar running across the wrist. It stuffs a
newspaper into the space in front of the *Vogue*s. "White
men," she says. He feels her shaking her head. "I don't even
want to think about it."

The boys—young men, really, in their early twenties, probably, but Kenneth's tongue is hanging (or would be, if he
didn't fear getting beat up) and the only word in his
thoughts is BOIIIZ, as his friend Cyrus would say it—the
boys have formed a delicate sphere of musk on the street
corner as they wait for the light to change.

Kenneth approaches slowly, groceries hanging in white
plastic from his hands. He fears to disturb them in any way.
His movement might stir a breeze and dispel the scent, and
the one bouncing the basketball against his drenched white
T-shirt might turn and see him, and know that Kenneth
has already stripped him bare and burrowed his wants-
to-be-hanging tongue into every crevice of his tanned,
lanky body.

If one is going to objectify men, and if one's objects, by chance or choice, are men of color, then it is going to be very difficult to salvage non-racist lust from altogether-too-racist darkskin = sexy-passionate desire: This is what Kenneth, postmodern intellectual of color, thinks to cool the stiffening in his pants as he draws near.

"Yo, man, I saw on the news this morning how a buncha Anglos beat the shit outta this puta and an African-American . . ." (he takes his time with this word; Kenneth cannot say whether he mocks or pays respect) " an then fuckin raped both of em, man. Can you believe that shit?" This one has a mustache and wears baggy cutoff sweatpants.

"Where? Bensonhurst?" Basketball-boy laughs.

"Nah, I think it was in the West Village or maybe Chelsea or someplace."

"Fuck," someone curses. Kenneth cannot see him.

"Well. You know. Like Jorgito say: Hey, sheet hawp-pen, man. Sheet hawp-pennn!"

Some laugh at the joke; others do not. By now they are crossing the street, taking their sweat and smell with them. One with thick black hair and a rusty complexion scowls back at the corner. Kenneth imagines that he was the one who cursed.

Kenneth frowns back. His erection no longer threatens.

The uptown subway train lurches more than Kenneth (who is now in a bad mood) thinks necessary, but at least it is not as crowded as it could be. He presses his back against the plastic orange seat and stares through the suit jackets draped over the arms of the men gripping the bar above his head.

"So what's the dish on Wendell?"

It is the queen sitting to Kenneth's left, whose big, tan hairy legs are dwarfed by the voluminous red socks that surround his ankles and make the flaps of his high-top tennis shoes bulge. Like his friend, who will give him the dish, he wears a short ponytail which, on frequent occasion (throughout this subway ride, anyway), he reaches back behind his head to stroke, like the tail of a poodle. Kenneth is pleased with neither of them.

"Oh, God. Wendell." Here the friend's voice grows hush. "You didn't hear he got attacked last week?"

"What?!"

"Yes, he went to Mars or Boybar or someplace—alone—and left late, and some Hispanic kids jumped him, called him a faggot and took his money. They slashed his arm and his chin, too."

"Oh, no!" The queen's hand comes up over his mouth in a child's gesture that wins Kenneth's sympathy. "Is he all right?"

"He's okay. It's happened to him before, except no one called him a faggot. But like I told him, those were all gay-bashings just the same, too. It never stops." The train stops and they rise, on nearly identical legs, and move toward the doors. "And when Carter found out, he was *furious,* I mean not just at—" The doors close again.

Kenneth's eyes are still squinted in sympathetic anger and concern when, casually, he notes the MAN RAPED page four headline box on the front of a *Post* someone has left behind. He looks away at the suit jackets, then looks back and arranges his grocery bags between his lower legs. He turns to page four.

When he sees the picture, it is as if someone has just injected his body with enough helium to float a dirigible.

* * *

The elevator in their building shudders to a start and jolts Kenneth's body back into its proper alignment. The building's conditioned air is cool, but his skin is still hot.

The sensation is exquisite and melancholic. It reminds Kenneth of his mother's kitchen, and summer afternoons of a childhood that could not possibly have been as frivolous and gloriously sunny as he remembers. But the memory, fiction or no, pleases him: he and his cousins racing about his parents' acre-large yard playing rough, raucous games until perspiration flowed down off of their foreheads like rain, and some responsible adult—an aunt, usually; his mother would be watching her soaps—would call them inside with the bribe of refrigerated sweets and car trips to the mall. They would burst into the vast white-and-blue kitchen, all greed and no manners, and plow through the proffered popsicles and ice cream sandwiches like little hurricanes, leaving sticky sticks and shameless drips of vanilla on the floor in their wake. But not one cousin, the eldest, tallest, and best mannered (and oddest, truth be told): he would often stand before the refrigerator, and open and close the freezer door while poking his head inside the smoky white fog until he was ready to sneeze. "The best part," he would tell his scoffing younger relatives. "Just wait till you get tall enough."

Once in their apartment, Kenneth drops his groceries and immediately picks up the phone.

INTERLUDE 2: KENNETH'S LATE SUMMER AFTERNOON DREAM: AT THE SIGN OF THE ASTRAL TATTOO

In Manhattan, shortly after it rains, in some places, there are tall streets. Dark and wet, and covered with small pools like flat eyes that reflect the shrouded gray sky, the asphalt, sidewalks and building facades flow together in continuous line, and the street attains height, like the rising of a mountain. The avenues do not have this power, and the effect is not at all the same as when, say, you fly just south of the island on a commuter plane at dusk and look out to see the streetlights spill onto the avenues, paving them with gold. No, that is mere appearance. This is fact: on tall streets, like the one this evening in Tribeca, there are dimensional portals.

This, then, is how it may have happened, according to at least one reputable conspiracy theory:

Inside the portal, Kenneth Gabriel became witness to a disquieting scene. *Witness,* I say, though he was not precisely divorced from its proceedings. He was a participant, in a sense, though his eyes were set in a body he did not altogether recognize. The disorientation was unsettling but it allowed him to enjoy the fragile luxury of disinterest, to say nothing of that threadbare savior of the West in the age of science, disbelief.

That said, Kenneth Gabriel walked on gangly legs in a lanky adolescent body over the cobblestones of a crooked street. He had on loose-fitting clothes with muted, basic colors, some khaki, some black, some white and a little blue—austere, pristine, unthreatening and impeccable. That seemed right.

His surroundings were a slightly different matter: smoke and the smell of burning meat gave a kind of brooding tension to the atmosphere, a feeling of warning and danger. On either side of the street leaned tilted buildings, like run-down versions of ancient Navajo pueblos. White sheets and black frocks hung from the sills of their dark windows, and when he passed, the old women who had been gossiping with one another on the doorsteps quickly covered their faces with red veils.

A man walked beside him. The man had his hand on Kenneth's shoulder. They were close, he and Kenneth. The man's face was split with a comic banana grin, and looking up Kenneth saw ingrown hair bumps along the man's cheeks. He seemed interested in comforting Kenneth.

Kenneth thought he might say something, but then they were no longer outside. They stood in a dark place with booths and tables arranged along a wall, and an L-shaped counter with a cash register at the near end stood before them. Kenneth sniffed and recognized the scent of oregano and feta cheese, and though the counter was bare, he thought he heard activity in the room beyond the open archway, where he saw a stove.

"Where are we?" Kenneth asked. It surprised him, a little, to learn that he actually could speak.

"This Zee's," the other man said. There was something familiar about him.

Suddenly—everything was sudden, here—a short, buxom woman came running out of the kitchen archway, clutching a loose blouse to her ample breasts. She was giggling, but as she raced past Kenneth her face wore an incongruous expression of fury.

"Who—?"

But now someone else was there, at the cash register. A rotund man with an olive complexion and great, bushy salt-and-pepper hair that seemed to flow into his long beard watched the woman go, his hands groping in her direction. Then he saw Kenneth and the other man.

He blew—not exhaled or sighed, but blew. Kenneth heard thunder. "Yeah?" the man said.

His hands dropped into the pockets of a blue bathrobe with a yellow lightning bolt drawn across its chest.

"We here for the Book of Names, Mr. Zee." It was the other guy talking. He seemed quite perky.

"Mm-hm." Zee looked bored and frustrated. He kept his eye on both of them while his hands rummaged for something below the countertop. "Christ! I *hate* this post!" he cried out, then looked skyward. He looked back at them. "He *never* answers."

Kenneth felt that he was beginning to understand.

Zee produced a small black book and took out a pen. "Names?"

"Hammett Wade," the other guy said. Kenneth looked up at him sharply.

"And you?" Zee said after a moment.

"Oh . . . I thought, I thought maybe you'd want to do him first."

"Look, boy, I did seventeen of you people just this morning. You know the rules. Two at a time minimum. Name?"

"But why should we go two at a time?" Kenneth asked. He was trying to keep pace with unfamiliar thoughts and wasn't sure what he meant by the question, though he felt certain that he had good reason to ask it.

"Special rules for ni—blacks."

"What? But isn't this appointment so we can get our destinies read to us? Isn't each destiny an individual thing?"

"Special rules for blacks."

"This is unfair!"

"Now, Kenny, baby, don't—!"

"Did I or did I not say special rules for blacks?"

"I refuse to go through with a bigoted interview process! Why should I?"

"Special. *Rules. For blacks.*" Zee began to see that his line of argument wasn't getting him anywhere. "Look, you don't think *I* want it this way, do ya? I mean, come on! This ain't my style at all! It's just the way things *are.* You seem like a smart guy, you know how it is. You know about Executive Order Number 3465255652565 of the actual *Original* Trilateral Commission, if you know who I mean." (Here he gave a confidential wink.) "I mean, even the Ghost was in on it, cause they made a deal, see, with Constantine.

Anyway: The Executive Order's terms are clear: Negative Action, sometimes called Negation Action, which compels those of us who hold these bullshit low-level administrative positions to play blacks in a zero-sum game. Tartarus, a *negative*-sum game, usually! The Order clearly states: Search out all those qualified to advance and impede their progress. In all things, two and three-quarters steps backward for every one step forward (it used to be three back for every one ahead, you know; the new Senate on High is more liberal, specially now that that zealot Michael is on vacation for a few centuries). In addition, if one goes up, *at least* one other goes down. No exceptions. See? My hands are completely tied.

"Now, naturally if it was just me, it'd be real different. I mean in the Old Country, when *we* ran things—before the economy got bad, you know, the general decline and everything, the coup by the generals, all that, and we hadda immigrate—when we ran it we would *never* have had such a system. I mean, a Book of *Names*? Please. We didn't bother keeping track of every little damn mortal, anyway. We had a lotta little figurines instead, like chess pieces, that that unattractive lame-boy smith made. You see that Ray Harryhausen movie *Clash of the Titans*? I *loved* it, and they made a good porn spoof of it, too, *Clash of the Tits*." Here he wiggled his big black-and-white eyebrows and grinned. "Porn's damn good. I like that best of all the developments in the last three hundred years. . . . But do you remember? Those little figurines Larry Olivier moved around? That's how we did it. But then, we was always much more concerned with physical *form* as opposed to *names,* because names have no substance. I mean, all this stuff about the flesh and the spirit divided and yayadeedeeya is so *annoying.*

You wouldn't catch us with any Book of *Names,* and we was much too busy fucking (ever had nymph pussy, fellas?— outta this world!) and fightin and feastin and drinking—me! them was the days!—but we was having such a good time, we never even thought of Executive Orders. And punishing a whole people? Never! A city, maybe. And even when we did that, we managed to salvage the guy who ended up founding Rome, right? No, we was *much* more civilized. We wouldn't think of this kind of arrangement against blacks! Hey, lemme tell you something, we got half our *stuff* from black Egypt. Which reminds me. Iris! Iris, send a memo up to personnel recommending old Ra or Amon or whoever the fuck he is today for my replacement at this post. Thank you, Iris. She's such a sweet old gal. Now, what was I—oh. Right. Now we didn't *call* it *black* Egypt, seeing as how nobody thought about these *color* matters like we do now. I mean, we had no racial prejudices whatsoever. Not too fond of barbarians, of course, but *Egypt!* If I get mine back—medammit, if those motherless fucks *had* balls, I'd take my papa's sickle and cut 'em right off! Well, no chance of that right yet. Still, though, this men's movement thing's got me very hopeful. Between Rob Bly and Joe Campbell . . . So, he's anti-Semitic? *You* try dealin with the old Unnamed I Am a Burning Damned Bush and see if you don't get a little upset! Now, now, I got nothin against ki—yer Jews, and I *don't* care that Dukakis married one, and besides the boys are delicious; yes, I do like boys, too, and if you'd seen that little cupbearer fella, you would, too. But *anyway.* With the men's movement, who knows in a couple hundred years? Beats the Tartarus out of feminism and all that *goddess* shit, I'll say that.

"Well, whatever. So: Ham Wade and who?"

"Uh, Kenneth Gabriel."

"Good. All right, then. I'll mark you down together. Now. Who gets the Successful Life Riddled With Self-Doubt, Disconnection From Community and Declining Sex Drive—*ewww*—and who gets Restless, Unloved Childhood followed by Obscure, Frustrated, Disrespected Manhood—*double ewww*—leading to Unexpected, Ignoble Death? You both get heaps of Indignities, of course."

Kenneth looked forward, Hammett down.

"Uh, I'll take the second one," Hammett said.

"But," Kenneth began. But he knew he wanted it that way.

"Give me your hands." They held out their hands. Zee turned them over and over, and then decided to put the stamps on their palms, where they would show up.

"Iris'll take you in the back room for the astral tattoos. Next!"

Through the looking glass, through a glass darkly, through thick and thin: stepping through the portal is like taking a step standing still. It's just not the same, all of a sudden (the *sudden* part—that doesn't change no matter where you are). Smooth, continuous lines become disjunct, contentious. There are no cobblestones, just gum wrappers and beer cans and little pieces of ugliness all over the street, and that's no Greek restaurant but a boarded-up shanty of a place with a wizened sign that says BARBER fading above what used to be a door. The rain whips through streets like this with the kind of misanthropy that could delight in drowning newborn babes, and there are no veiled women to stoop on the doorsteps and make you feel better because they, too, know how disheartening it all is and may give you a glance of sympathy if you pass near (but not too near) them. There is no brooding tension, nothing foreboding in the atmosphere. There is no need: all dire predictions have long since come to pass.

This evening in Tribeca, on a tall street, Kenneth Gabriel ducks his head against the rain and knows that this is the place where you have to get up high and fly just south, so that you can see the gold.

PART TWO

LATER...

10

THE ADVENTURES OF EVAN MARCIALIS

"Hey!" The place has a funny smell.

"Hey! I just had the *best* time with Vicki. She's hilarious. You *have* to meet her. . . ."

In the dark his face is cold blue like the TV screen. He waves two fingers without speaking and his eyes don't move. Theatrical. I hug him from behind and bury my nose in his neck. There's a McDonald's bag at his bare feet. "I thought you were gonna make a salad for dinner."

"You've been drinking," he says, hugging back.

"Yeah, we taped late again, then Vicki and Drew wanted to go have drinks and I went along. We had a blast. What're you watching?"

"You smell nice. I like beer breath." His eyes look really big in the TV light.

"Thanks . . . Who's that—that morning talk show woman?"

"Yeah, she's doing a special on career women with babies. Like her."

Uh oh.

"Everytime I see her I think: this is what fascism American style'll look like. This is its *face*—blond hair, blue eyes, good white smiles while you chat with the good white day-care teacher—although they did manage to throw in this officious-looking black couple from Scarsdale who look like *Ebony* cigarette ad models."

Something's coming. Has to be.

"Meanwhile my cousin gets raped and killed in the fucking *street*! TV will look just the same when we're in concentration camps."

"What? What cousin? What happened?"

All of a sudden it seems like, his eyebrows are pulled tight together, the skin around his eyes twisted. So much pain. You can feel it.

"Remember that news report you told me about yesterday?" he says, loud. "The man who got raped? The one you *fantasized* about? Well, he has a name. Hammett Wade. He was my cousin."

(KENNETH WATCHES: I said that too nastily. Like it's his fault. I don't even see him, really, or hear him. Just a blank pale face I see, and I hear a high, shrill whistle.)

"Read this." He hands me a newspaper. BLACK MAN RAPED RESCUING PROSTITUTE. I skim while Kenneth goes off.

"I didn't even know! I just happened to pick it up on

the subway coming back from St. Mark's! There was no one to tell me, no friends in common . . ." He passes his hand over his face, breathes hard. "Can you believe it?" he starts up again. He sounds so—desperate. "They *raped* him. He saw them gang raping some poor prostitute and I guess he yelled at them or something according to what they're able to get out of the woman, and then they chased him, beat the fuck out of him, and then since God knows it's not enough to beat up a black man they fucked him like he was a blow-up doll or something. They raped him."

"Where did this happen?" Stupid question; it's probably right there in the article. I don't know what to say, what I'm saying.

"Who the *fuck* cares where?! Why does everybody's great-grandmother want to know *where*? What is this, another oh-he-shouldna-been-there thing? I mean, this was a lynching—does it matter whether it's North or South?"

"Okay, Kenneth!" I shouldn't have snapped. "You know that's not what I meant. I just wondered because there've been a lot of gay-bashings down in the Village in the past month and maybe the same crew is raping hookers and killing black men, too." I know that's ridiculous, but what am I supposed to say? "Is it okay if I ask *when* it happened?"

He glares up at me for the sarcasm but answers anyway. "I guess about a week and a half ago. The woman apparently managed to tell the police some part of the story after she got to a hospital, and they took their sweet time getting to the scene to check it out. Then he wasn't there, and they couldn't find him for a while because they didn't have a description. Then they got some weird anonymous tip, and went back out there and found him in some alley

around the corner from where it happened. Daria told me
that one of the reporters from her paper said that the police
had supposedly seen his body before, but they assumed he
was some homeless drunk. Can you believe that? Lying
there in the alley lynched!"

"Did they actually lynch him?" I feel totally weird,
hollow but just *weird,* and almost—well, not sexually, but
kind of excited in some bizarre way.

Kenneth's finger snaps at a button on the remote and
screenlight flashes like lightning. "He was left tied up and
dead, and a gang of white men did it. Substitute the fact
that they raped him for a castration and except for the
fact that he wasn't hanging from a tree, it sounds like a
lynching to me."

"Oh, my God." I put my arm back around him. "And
he was your cousin?"

"He's my uncle's wife's son. We used to call him our
cousin-in-law."

"So you knew him pretty well? You never told me you
had a cousin in New York."

(KENNETH WATCHES: He wants to reach me, but he
is not sure. His touch is tentative, guarded. He is
not sure whether what he will reach is the thing
white people fear. I'm not sure, either. Perhaps in
a moment a metamorphosis will be triggered. My
skin and flesh will collapse, melt and reform as a
compact mass of pitch-black, wiry hair and sheets
of powerful muscle. I'll grow cropped ears and a
nubbed tail and paws with iron claws, and I'll
leap and catch and crush his head, his splendid
square-jawed head, between great white fangs.

Perhaps he'll touch some secret, tender place on my skin and find not love or desire or vulnerability. Only fury. Only rage. And hate, and murder.)

"I haven't talked to Hammett since I first moved here. We're not close."

"Oh."

Kenneth is stiff, hugging himself sort of. Like back off, leave me alone. But he needs me, I know, and so I hug him a little tighter, rest my hand lightly on his. I try again. "Well, this sounds awful, I know, but the way New York is today, at least if it's racially motivated maybe it'll get some press, and that might help them catch the people who did it. Not like just another gay-bashing or another rape between two people of the same race."

"I don't know if that's true. And it was a gay-bashing."

"He was gay?" I thought so. "Do the police know? I mean, did it say so in the article?"

Kenneth makes a noise, like he's disgusted. "No, they just mentioned that he was an *ex-soldier* and that he's been a mailman in Brooklyn for five years. I don't know where that soldier emphasis came from. Sounds like something my father would mention."

"Did your father know he was gay?"

"He suspected, probably. Dad started suspecting everyone who wasn't married or with a girlfriend after I came out. He started looking at us with that worried face he inherited from my grandmother." Kenneth makes a face. "I even caught him reading my little brother's journal. And he would ask all these questions of my male cousins when they'd come home from college for the summer. Of course it never occurred to him that anyone might be a lesbian, like his very own aunt. Hammett left for Brooklyn not long after the time I decided to come out. Which was also not very long after we slept together."

"You slept with him?" I hope that didn't sound horrified or anything. I'm just kind of excited.

(KENNETH WATCHES: This is all cover conversation, of course. Pretty plastic wrapping for spoiled, rotten meat. Safe. I'm still furious.)

"It wasn't a big thing. I mean it was my first real grown-up homosexual experience, I guess, but . . . He was seven years older and I sort of knew he had his eye on me, and I guess I was ready. I just remember being excited by his obviousness—you know: You're so fine and beautiful, sweet thing, I just want to lick all the sweet sweat off your tight body and let me introduce you to my love machine blah blah blah. He was sleazy, kind of. I always thought so, even when he was in the army and would come back with all that cologne on those silk shirts and talk, talk, talk. But I was ready and so I got excited about everything about him."

He seems more relaxed now, so I ask, "Do you really think this was a gay-bashing, though? It seems like these guys went after him because he tried to rescue that woman."

"Who knows? I don't know exactly how to think about it. I don't know how you really talk about it. What incensed and excited them more—that he was black, gay, black and gay? Did they know he was gay, and how could they think they knew he was gay if they did? Maybe he'd cruised one of them earlier in the evening. I think he had some sort of thing for white boys."

We both look down quickly, then back up. Did Kenneth notice?

He pauses. I put my hand on his shoulder again. It's warm. "Is there something I can do for you, maybe take your mind off this a little?"

For a second it seems there's a skeptical, dismissive expression on his face. Like he's saying: You can do something about *this*? And I suddenly feel stupid. His disbelief makes me disbelieve. But now he just shakes his head. "No. Thanks. I need to call my father again anyway."

"Okay." I consider for a second before I ask, "Do you think you might tell your dad Hammett was gay? Or tell the press if they don't know?"

"I don't know. I'll have to think about it, talk to people. But not right now."

I lift his hand and kiss it. "I'd be happy to talk with you about it."

"Thank you." Kenneth sounds like he's here now, talking to me. "I'll look you up." He laughs.

In a while it seems all right to break the mood, so I get up, look at the clock and go to the bathroom to brush my teeth.

The water is running, but I hear voices and music. He's putting off calling his father, I guess. "What're you watching now?" I call out.

"*Star Trek*—the old one. It's 'Return of the Archons,' where the computer controls everyone on the planet and allows them to go crazy and be violent and have sex only once a month, or once a week or something." He sounds drained now, and small.

I walk out of the bathroom and without saying anything we start folding out the couch bed together. Kenneth buffs the sheets with his hand; I go for the pillows in the closet.

On the way back I glance at the TV. "Oh, it's almost over! This is the part where he tells the computer that it fucked up because it made a culture where there's no free will, and it's harming people instead of helping them the way it's programmed to. Kirk always pulls this trick. Speak illogic to a computer and it blows up. Wouldn't that be great, if we could change society that way—just go to the master computer and tell it nothing makes sense, and then the whole power structure would collapse?"

"Yeah," Kenneth says. He throws off his pants and slips under the covers. "Yeah, that would be nice."

In my first dream tonight, I'm an ensign on the *Enterprise,* and Captain Kirk asks me to his quarters and then bends over and tells me to stick it where no man has been before.

. . . Later on I wake up to go to the bathroom. I pull my dick out from my boxers and point it carefully because sometimes I shoot wide when I'm sleepy. So I'm trying to hold it steady, but I keep moving it because something isn't right. It doesn't look right to me. My dick looks different. And then—really weird, almost like déjà vu—I remember that when I pulled it out to screw Kirk that it was long, thick, and black.

11

SNAKE EYES AND THE WHITE GIRLS

KENNETH WATCHES: This morning I awoke with a headache. My tongue felt dry and fat in my mouth, and I longed for something sweet but not heavy or too rich—a childish yearning for gardens where lilac flowers smell of cinnamon and baked apple, and the leaves are covered with brown sugar pollen or a light smear of white frosting. I wanted cereal the way I used to have it as a little boy, when my cousin Cara and I got up on Saturday mornings just before seven to watch the reruns of *Superman* before the real cartoons came on—cereal of purple, pink, and orange shapes that I slurped hungrily from a shallow spoon until the best part: the discolored, sugar-laden milk that I drank straight from the bowl, like an Amazon savage (so I excitedly imagined) drinks blood. Sweet like that.

That was what I wanted this morning, rolling around with my headache beneath the covers.

When I finally got up, Evan was gone (of course; why

would he not be gone?) and the post-rain sun was high and bright outside the window. The window needs cleaning, I thought, but I'm no housewife. (Funny I should remember that thought now, an hour later. It still nettles. I must be feeling resentful.) And my memory got better as I chewed on a hunk of rough eighteen-hundred grain wheat bread.

Cousin Cara? There was no cousin Cara. Cara was the black Barbie doll Daria got and didn't much like one Christmas when we were about ten. I liked Cara. She was coffee-colored and had long hair, like the black Wonder Woman in DC Comics who wore a short leopard-spotted skirt and was my ideal of feminine beauty. Cara's hair wasn't as long, though; they tried to be authentic and gave it a rough texture, which I sort of liked and sort of didn't.

Daria didn't bother with the sort-ofs. She didn't like Cara and gave her to me two days after New Year's. Our parents teased us that Daria and I were girlfriend and boyfriend, but we were just friends, period (how could I be boyfriend to a girl without long Wonder Woman hair? of course I got over that white standard of beauty thing after freshman year in college). Daria liked dolls, but not as much as I (sort of/a little bit/excitedly) did. She gave me Cara, and in the basement when Mom was at work and my sister was at my grandmother's and my brothers were out playing football in one of the yards up the street, Cara met my G.I. Joes, fell madly in love and demanded to be taken on adventures with them. She may even have been—and this part is shameful—she may have been, as time went on, and as we boys in the neighborhood discovered the tantalizing sin of pornography, ravished a time or two.

I might still have Cara somewhere—probably still wrapped up and elaborately concealed beneath three dozen more appropriate toys in a box of stuff Mom keeps (for her grandchildren, she says) in the basement. The terror that Mom would find it! Or worse, Dad. I used to make up lies in advance: Daria left it here; I needed it for school (which would never have worked); it belongs to cousin-in-law Hammett. That one might have worked; everyone knew Hammett was odd and an untrustworthy liar. Of course it would have been a betrayal of Hammett, a thought that didn't trouble me as much as it ought. . . .

Well.

Since extricating myself from the siren lures of late morning delusions I have been trying to read a biography of Paul Robeson, but my headache keeps closing my eyes. I am weary of the couch (laugh: the thin-lipped, ivory-skinned blue blood woman in silk bathrobe with fur trimming eating bon-bons in the living room rises languidly and gestures to the butler, *"Chester, take it away. I am weary of the couch."*).

I go over to the window and open it. The city smells fresh. The rain yesterday left us an unexpected moment of peace, a deep, green, ancient quiet that must have given even the brutal European colonizers pause when they arrived upon New World shores.

I think I shall select a novel from my shelf of unread classics—the kind I like, one about the desultory states of being—and take it out with me to the Park (no new listings at the university today, but I should check the papers).

I am not in the mood for inhabitation. There is something—a small thing, maybe, like Evan left a bowl in the sink, soiled with two broken cornflakes in two drying, greasy clumps of white yogurt clinging to the side of the bowl, knowing as he must know that it would *enrage* me.

Or: I have to meet Cyrus for lunch and I know that queen is going to give me his attitude, and I'll have to tell him about Hammett. . . . But no, that's not it. There is something blocking the way. I cannot gather myself, collect myself enough to scatter, to voyage out.

From my window—it is not high; we are favored, by Evan's money and my fortuitous connections with a peripatetic friend, with a second-floor efficiency that looks out upon a one-block park (not *my* park; I seldom visit this one), and I can see its patrons clearly—I can see their faces, though I cannot hear their voices. And among them, no doubt, are souls, shapes, looks and hairstyles which I might inhabit, if I could. Which might nourish.

This one, for instance. There is a look about him of which I am not fond. It resides in his upper eyelids, which in combination with the slight puff of the bags beneath his eyes are too large by half and evoke my fear of the reptilian. I could, I am sure, discover all manner of things about him, about that snake-eyed look, but I cannot make too much of this, for as likely as not my reaction stems from something as silly as a television show villain, some late-night movie I saw as a child or, perhaps, as a self-loathing adolescent, searching for things with which to be more disgusted than myself.

But then of course he waves at the fake blonde (brazenly so; she makes no effort to conceal her blaring brown roots) with the black skirt and the fish lips, who has just been joined at the picnic table by a real blonde with a handsome face and an expression at the rim of her nostrils of pinched distaste. I think the two women do not like one another—see how often they lean away from the table and toss back their tresses; they use their hair like shields—but that is only a guess. In any case they make no great pretense of being bosom friends. There is no hypocrisy in their little union out there on the grass, but rather an easy, familiar distance, as if they were both part of some elite sorority that tolerates all its members only because its number is so few. I wanted to call them White Girls at first, and sneer. But, though they undoubtedly once were and can still be, I suspect now that they are not, have ceased to be, and have warily entered a passionless, packaged variant of White Womanhood with which they are uncomfortable but which is too comfortable to abandon.

No. It doesn't take. I skim too quickly, and the surfaces are too difficult to penetrate, too easy to sidestep. There is nothing *physical* there upon which I can get my hands; those eyes, those brazen roots—like finding only saucers in the cupboard when one craves a bowl of cereal.

Perhaps that's what I'll do, go out and buy a box of cereal. For there is something in the way: a small thing, maybe, ephemeral, evanescent like a moment of déjà vu.

I close the window, and let it rule.

. . . Today today I inhabit a headache.

12

KENNETH AND CYRUS AT LUNCH

"Fwoinne," Cyrus purrs, red-brown eyebrows arched over cat-eye sunglasses.

I follow his gaze. "Serious fwoin," I agree when I see him.

"Ummnh." Cyrus shakes his head, almost imperceptibly, just enough for me to see. "Positively strapping." He savors the consonants in that way of his that surprises the muscles of my face by the breadth of the smile it cajoles. My laugh is already beginning. "And look at his friend."

His friend saunters by in a thin-strapped, deeply-plunging tank top, and the muscles of his back show, exquisitely sculpted in the sunshine. "Oh my," I intone.

"It almost makes me want to move back to Manhattan," Cyrus says reverently, leaning back in his chair. He lifts a crouton from his salad to his mouth. There is such a style about him even as he does this small thing—overblown, perhaps, just a tad too consciously flamboyant (*too* if we take an Anglo-Saxon norm of "restraint" in all things as our guide—I remind myself of the injustice of this), but dead on. Always. "Some of these b-boys who come around here are the Bomb."

Now I laugh. The Bomb. Precisely. I haven't heard that one before.

"So, my sweet—" (This is what he calls me. He may flatter any number of his friends with the same endearment, but I am always made happy by it, confirmed by it, gathered by it into a grateful communion. I met Cyrus one night through a woman friend I was in a play with, and over hurried drinks at a cafe I came breathlessly to the decision that he was both charming and dangerous, delightful but intimidating, much too sure of himself for me to want to know too well. But weeks later he did a reading of his poetry at a Gay and Lesbian Performance Night and dazzled me with his warm, open assumption of community. I didn't quite buy it, of course—brotherhood, I thought; where's mine? But he made me desperate to believe. I have been chasing his friendship ever since.)

But let me step out of the way, let him speak.

"—there's a new performance piece we're putting on at the theater," he is saying. "It's more of a one-act play than anything else, and I thought you might want to audition."

Suddenly I feel the possibility of a depression flying at me. But let me step out of the way. "What's it called? What's it about?"

Cyrus waves a fork—swallowed clean, of course—at my face; it is the imperial director in him. "Don't play this, Kenneth. Don't start retreating to that oh-it's-a-*black*-thang remove you run to everytime I ask you to audition for one of my shows. No, I'm serious! It is time to *wake up,* little boy." He pounces quickly, as always. Of course I admire his technique. "That's right: *lit-tle boy.* Kenneth, I'll tell you this like I've told you before. You need to stop pouting. You need to start making use of the contacts you have. You can't keep pulling yourself back and stopping before you begin. You have *talent.* You have to *use* it."

"I'm not good at black dialect. I'm just not."

Cyrus rolls his eyes hugely. "Kenneth, that was one audition and one play, and one director. And she was right: traditional black folk's English is not your strength. You sound—a little forced, a little . . . shaky. There are, however, a good number of plays out there with middle-class, bougie Aframericans in them that you *can* play, and play well." Having been hunched, his broad, slim shoulders (they give him such carriage, those; were he a woman, he would have been a model in Paris, smooth swinging boyish hips, pursed lips and all) fall down and he relaxes, a smirk on his lips. This is how he plays with me.

"Phallicist's honor, Kenneth." He places two fingers in a V on either side of his nose, like Agnes Moorehead in *Bewitched.* We share a devotion to Agnes's memory, Cyrus and I. "I really think you could play a number of parts in this piece very, very well. I even told the director you might be a good choice for the lead."

I meet this with silence because I am terrified. Principally terrified of disappointing Cyrus. He is waiting impassively for my reply, golden-skinned face set in quiet judgment. "Can I see a script?" I ask at last.

"They can make a copy for you at the *GMOC Journal* office—the Lesbian/Gay Community Center, third floor." But of course he knows I know this. He has seen me lurking there a number of times.

Now a new silence looms. This is not typical of our conversations, and he must know this. I sip my tea while he watches me. It is a contest of wills now.

Cyrus breaks first. "Uh," he says. This degree of inarticulation is also not typical. "I, uh, heard about your cousin."

The roll I am lifting to my mouth I set back in the basket. "What? Who told you?"

"Daria. She didn't say much," he adds quickly. "I'm really sorry, Kenneth. And I have to say, I feel it, too, a part of it, even though I didn't know him. I remember you mentioned him once." He sighs, shakes his head, looks across the street. "So many perils are out there for our people in this city, Kenneth. If it's not run-of-the-mill cracker bigots, it's homophobic cracker bigots, and if it's not homophobic cracker bigots, it's Jamaican homophobe bigots or Puerto Rican bigots or run-of-the-mill black folks homophobic bigots. Then if it's not men who think beating you to death is a sport that helps them prove something precious to themselves, it's sistas who think that because your penis is black it belongs to them in holy wedlock, or who, if they can't get your penis, know you must be using it to steal their men. Then the police, the government . . . I mean, you know all this. I just want you to know that it pains me, too. It really does. And not just for you but for myself."

He shakes his head again, more vigorously. I don't think I've ever seen him quite this way, his passion expressed like this. His glasses obscure his eyes like clouds before the sun. "I'm sorry," he says, and touches my hand. "I just keep talking. Do you—want to talk about it?"

I had envisioned, practiced this conversation earlier.

But I am not as smooth, as nonchalant as I had hoped to be when I say, "I think I saw him."

I have not said this aloud before. My throat is constricted. "He was walking around, I think, near Different Light bookstore, before it happened. I had just left there, I was walking on one of those little streets behind the bookstore, and I heard someone call my name, and I looked back. I think it was him."

"You didn't speak?" There is no judgment in the question.

"No." There is more to say. "No. No."

"I *hope* you're not thinking you're to blame for his being killed because you didn't *speak* to the man. Cause, child, if every relative I wasn't speaking to at any given time dropped dead, I'd be an orphan by now."

I fake a small smile. I've thought of this, of course. Yet it gives me hope to hear it from his lips.

He smiles back. "The universe is not that bleak, Kenneth. It's not *that* cruel."

This time there is nothing more to say.

But Cyrus will not permit any more silences. "So how's Mr. Marcialis? Being a good boy, I hope?" This with a mock Caribbean lilt in his voice. I marvel at his cleverness—not the accent, but the connection he's discerned, the link that, in a few words, he has uncovered.

"Yes. Mostly," I answer. My turkey sandwich tastes like paper. The sigh comes; he has already—the sorcerer—dragged it out of me. "It's very hard, Cyrus. Very hard sometimes to . . ."

The fingertips of his hand reach out to rest upon the veins that stand out on the back of my exposed arm. "To love a white boy?" And there is about him a smug but sympathetic certainty, as if his other hand were slowly stroking a sinister goatee at the end of his chin.

"Yes, it's hard." I exhale. "But harder—I don't know; is it harder? just as hard—not to. It's what we're taught, you know, to love them. Even in hate. Hate's just another way to love someone. It's just safer because you don't really need to know them."

He stares at me. One of his brutish fingers circles my thumb in a loving vise. The sensation is of the vampire drawing the bared and willing neck tenderly to his lips, or of the Godfather, pulling an errant Family member's frightened face to his own for the last kiss.

"Kenneth. You are completely, absolutely wrong." This as if he were blowing in my ear.

And now his finger leaves mine, his breath (scented, faintly, with the cinnamon-orange iced tea he has been drinking) leaves my face, his torso recedes from the top of the small white table.

"Your problem, my sweet, is not with white boys or even white men." His fork is raised high for a brief second, tines to the sky. "It's with The Folks." The fork descends and a crouton flies. "Aframerican male Folk to be specific. So it's hard loving white men, is it? Not really, little boy. You don't love white *men;* you happen—as much as anything can just happen, I suppose—to be in love with one white *man.* And you might have loved one in the past, may love another in the future. Of course you're attracted to them, but not every one every day, or even most of the time. I know you, Kenneth. Your desires—like everybody else's, one way or another, and don't let them fool you, baby, because it's true—but your desires are not such that you run around with your tongue hanging out and following after every pale swimmer with a chlorine bleached-out blond crewcut and eyes that look green in bad light.

"Don't laugh! I've seen it happen, and it's funny, but it's not pretty. That's not where you are. Your problem is that you've set yourself up so that the only men you *can* love are white men—and I'll include Latinos, Asians, native Americans, and Semitic Folk in there, too, because anyone that ain't Folks is white in your little love em or leave em no middle ground no complications moral world.

"Don't argue! I only read for the benefit of the person being read, so just keep your little ass still in that chair and listen. It's black men or any other kind of man for you, right? Either or. You never felt comfortable, never liked or felt liked by all those beautiful, sexy, heterosexual Aframerican men who ran around, beloved by all, talkin bout playin ball and gettin pussy and my woman this and your woman that. Right? You hated them. Admit it. *Hate.* That's how you felt, because they were supposed to belong to you, make you belong, right? And they didn't. And *don't*—mostly. So you don't love them, sometimes still hate em. And you think because of that that maybe you don't really love The Folks at all and feel terribly guilty when you read some writer talking about how much he or she loves Our People. Right?

"But this is the thing, Kenneth: You do love The Folks. You love Aframerican women, right? How many times do we sit here and sing their individual praises? Hm? And you never knew a black gay man—that was *out*—before you came to New York. Right? You've convinced yourself that you hate you and hate The Folks, too, but like my grandmother down South used to say, It don't make no kinda sense, baby. And it don't. You *love* you. Somewhere

that's true; otherwise you wouldn't be here, alive and
healthy, today. Too many of us don't know how to love our-
selves and don't make it, even out of safe bougie
Aframerica. You love you. And you love *us,* The Folks.
There are plenty of us out here, out there, that aren't those
boys you hated and still hate now. Women, Aframerican gay
men. And I would be willing to say, even a good number of
those boys that you hate and fear so much. See? All that
love is right there, waiting for you."

I see this finger—looks huge—like a gun barrel
pointed at my chest.

"And Kenneth—in whatever way, however much, even
if it doesn't seem in hindsight like it was enough—you
loved your cousin. You did. And you have to really know
that, believe it. It almost has to show up in your dreams for
it to be real."

And now he leans back. The smug sympathetic sinister
goatee stroking expression returns. "I'd snap," he says
blandly, "but I'm too tired." He really does have a beauty
about him.

We are silent.

I'm a stubborn man, I'll admit, and being read does
not sit well with me. With confessed vengefulness, then, I
can only say that it seems to me that I shall never be able
to bring myself to obey one word of his advice, not one
whit of it. *It has to show up in your dreams,* he said. That is
what plays in my head now, as he asks, "How're the
Games?"

He is teasing, but I cannot answer. "Fine," is all I say.
And then: "How's your thing?"

"Oh—!" Another fork flourish. "Good. The fucking is

delicious. Makes me so thankful I'm a phallicist." My laugh is beginning again; the smile is already there.

"The problem, of course, is that he's a *man*—as unoriginal a thing as *that,* and men have unfortunately all been taught, whatever their race"—he shoots me a look; his lover is black—"that they have something to *say* about things. Which is ridiculous, because most men haven't anything at all to say about most things, unless it's offensive or forgettable. Or *stupid.* Women are better life partners, ultimately. They're taught they have nothing to say, and consequently they have *everything* fascinating and insightful to say, because they kept quiet or pretended to keep quiet and they learned something, and didn't burble out their entire brainload before age ten. *But*—!" He smiles, as pleased with himself as I am. "Men do have penises."

And we both laugh.

Later, I am watching him recede from me as I stand at the corner, his slim shoulders carrying him, his step bouncing him gently away, like a little buoy bobbing slowly up and down in a sea of bodies and chatter.

Why do I find it so easy to love Cyrus?

13

A STORY OF EVAN

KENNETH WATCHES: He is asleep, and I watch over him, an unlikely guardian angel, unclothed and lustful. It is the memory of our lovemaking that keeps me awake, that keeps me propped here on one elbow, fixated upon the side of his face illuminated by gentle blue moonlight.

Men are boys, and never more so than when they are asleep (or, perhaps, at war, but my Evanitch is too much the pacifist for that). Asleep, his lips, pink and small, part, his lower lip like a slackened drawbridge. Inside there is a dark tunnel, and caverns and passageways and trap doors, and a secret chamber, maybe, where his soul sits and trembles as he dreams. I could enter, if I willed. Asleep, men are vulnerable.

But it is the memory that keeps me awake. I cannot simply lie still and savor my orgasm, cannot rise with its high-floating calm and then settle down to dream within its silken folds. I do not linger with orgasms. Always I must be *up,* in some fashion or another. Must pee, must clean up, must must must. Tonight I must remember. I must record and recall everything we did and how it felt—the quiver of his touch, the smell of his sigh at my nostrils, the taste of the hair on the underside of his arm.

For there was something different. A purity. A window into something. And that—not a mere orgasm—is to be treasured. Especially now, tonight, when the window has darkened and he has become so much flesh, blood, and human foible, and especially these days, when my dreams no longer inhabit him as they once did.

Upon a time, when the name Evan Marcialis carried with it the deep tremor of repressed obsession, I could not have a fantasy in which he did not figure. I watched him one day, when chance or something like it took me to a Picasso exhibit on a sweltering afternoon. In the museum gift shop I leafed through an overpriced book of photographed paintings and looked up, then looked away. I didn't *want* to look. I did not like blonds. But of course I looked. He was not as he appears now, a pale boy on a moonlit mattress. He wore a black T-shirt tucked into small black athletic shorts, and the fine hairs on his fine, sinewed legs matched in hue and visual texture those on his arms. He wore dark sunglasses and walked with an occasional totter, as if off balance.

It was the totter and the sunglasses which caught me. He reached behind his glasses to rub a reddened eye, and I saw him bellowing in the night, stumbling drunken with friends out of a club at four A.M., winding his way through the streets to the apartment of a friend who was not his lover. They stopped at an all-night market and stood by the cookie and cracker shelf and giggled—the sort of giggle that catches in your throat and prevents you from breathing, a giggle that is still a laugh years later when it is recalled and returns you to a forgotten intimacy.

The two of them—he, the friend, was a nerdish geology student who had just come out and thought that to be gay was to wear no underwear and to work out at the gym—fell upon the shag-carpeted floor and into an uninhibited two-man orgy that ended an hour later, with the geology student draped over the back of a couch wondering what they had done with the pillows and figuring that if he'd just been exposed to the AIDS virus it had been worth it.

Later Evan slunk out, taking time only to comb his hair with his fingers and, having found his pants in a rather embarrassing state, to rifle through the sleeping geology student's dresser drawer for some shorts, which he found and put on, though they were too small and accentuated his crotch more than he might have liked. He had brunch plans with an ex-girlfriend and was already late, so instead of going home he bought some cheap sunglasses at a stand outside the bus station. Being late, he couldn't object when his ex insisted that he buy her a drink, and then since she refused to drink alone he ordered a tall mimosa—which, now in the museum gift shop, he regretted.

All this I lived (some details I filled in later, alone in my bed) before he waved his hand (the gesture was a bit effeminate, appealingly so) at the bald man behind the counter, gesturing toward a colorful poster. When he left, I trailed discreetly behind and saw him playfully smack his rolled-up poster over the head of a curly-haired guy in worn khakis and a faded rugby shirt who was seated outside on the steps. *Smack!* he brought it down over the man's head, and then he laughed, and curly hair chased him down the steps, and I lost myself in the envy and exploration of that *smack!,* of the whole history of their tumultuous, playful relationship. (Curly hair had been his freshman year roommate, and it was he who had broken Evan up with his ex-girlfriend, and . . .)

Then, Evan was sex and love and every moment of intimacy I missed or never had, but wanted. In his presence I leapt beyond myself.

Now he is asleep: a little boy with a little mouth, marvelous, unknowable, but contained.

And I am awake.

Tonight I (remember how I used to) inhabit my lover.

What made it so easy to love him, then?

14

THE GAY SONS OF HAM

KENNETH WATCHES: Cyrus, Daria and I are walking. Around us, the humid night is crowded with color, everyone in sight attired as if for a Bacchanalian revel. My eyes blur with gaudy violets, screaming oranges, overripe cherry scarlets, flagrant shades of violet and green. In this crowd blue is not mere blue but ultra-ultramarine: the sight of it, wrapped around those hips, that chest, and all those legs, sends ripples through me. Opulence sidles by in a teal silk blouse that rustles against silvered white pearls in the breeze. Decadence makes itself known in a pair of banana-yellow gym shorts with symmetrical furrows radiating from either side of a supply curved crotch. (Why this is decadence I cannot say—but there is a stain on the shorts, just where the flared cockhead would be, if he wears it at a slight left-and-down tilt. I *love* that stain.) The cars—even the cars announce themselves with idiosyncratic flair—they whistle past like space-age flight trams and leave brief, twinkling tails of light behind, like wisps of stardust.

I look out upon this fairy-play and am transported elsewhere. (I can't help myself; I love a thing and my love for it takes me beyond it: compelling presences compel still more poignant presences, as a melancholy absence cries out for a created, vivifying presence.) So I am deposited among other blurs, of golden streetlights washing over golden stone walls on a hot, hot August night in Madrid. I am eleven and my family is chattering in confusion about directions to the hotel, while I'm chafing to be free of them and to sprint away at full speed and down gold and night-blue streets and shout my paean to the stars.

Cyrus and Daria are elsewhere.

("Child," Cyrus drawls. "There are *hella* tourists here."

"And all those tacky colors," Daria agrees. "How do you stand living here, Kenneth?")

Think of it this way—as Carnival. Think that you are in Rio or Venice or Trinidad, and everyone is masked and painted and dancing maniacally. That's how I'm going to think of it.

("But I still don't know if I understand your point, Daria," Cyrus says. He is continuing an argument and adjusts the right lens of his glasses with thumb and forefinger to communicate this. "In the milieu of the play, lesbianism as a concept just doesn't work for the characters. Esperanza and Margarita have sex because they're close friends and love each other, but they're in an environment or a situation where actually choosing to *say* that they're dykes or bisexuals doesn't really occur to them."

"Well, I object to that," Daria says. The hair at the top of her fade prickles under the lights. "If they don't embrace the identity, their sexuality becomes just a function of being outré. They become just these young, punk, under-class Latina exotics in a zoo. They're just more, I don't know, decadent for an audience that's probably largely homophobic."

"How can you say that? What do you know about the audience? I mean—!")

The thing about the play that stays with me is one winter scene where the two women sleep on the couch in a friend's apartment. Fully clothed they pull a Scottish tartan blanket over themselves up to their necks and lie together in the cold, still as broomsticks. There is no other furniture on the stage. Then, with a tinkling sound that slowly builds into a rattle, a steam radiator cranks into action. The women sigh and relax beneath the blanket, and then the lights slowly go down. In the darkness the only sound in the theater is the noise of the radiator, jangling like a chain of housekeys held in your lover's hand as he shuts the apart-ment door upon his return from a late night at work; creak-ing, like a roommate's wincing step on noisy floorboards after midnight. That was how I felt it, as friendship and home and love beneath a blanket, and that was why I could feel the warmth rising from the radiator's coils. A distilled moment, as only theater can deliver it. I liked the play, for giving me that.

("It is hilarious that you're arguing this point given your position on the whole Hammett thing!" Daria's voice rises. Journalists love to argue.

"Daria, that is completely different—!"

"Oh, art is one thing, politics another, right?"

"My point, Madame Koppel"—he does his thing with the consonants; I smile—"has to do with *effectiveness,* and whether art or politics the analysis doesn't change. The play worked tonight without using the term lesbian. It may have worked *because* it didn't use the term. Whatever: the message got across. All I'm saying to you and to Kenneth is that beatings, lynchings, shootings, whatever kind of mayhem against Aframerican men is old everyday news and in order to draw proper attention to it you need a good media hook. We have always got to repackage the struggle."

Daria thrusts her arm across Cyrus's stomach to stop him from marching into a taxi before she says, "I don't see how people knowing Hammett was gay packages anything in a way people could care less about. If anything, it'll make it seem like he *wanted* it, or deserved it, because this was a sexual murder. Plus, lynching black men may be old news, even in New York, but so is gay-bashing, if it was ever news at all."

"Right!" A thick finger wags. "But if we draw attention to Hammett as a lynched *black gay* man, maybe we could get some coverage, at least from the black and gay presses. This is an opportunity to raise important questions and for our community to be seen—!")

Seen: The images multiply like rabbits—or orcs or tribbles, if your name is Evanitch Marcialis and the referents for your universe are Tolkien and *Star Trek.* But anyway the images multiply: they become a cacophony of black talking heads arrayed on a pyramid of television sets in an electronics store display window. The heads, latter-day versions of the Benin, are colored a variety of shades from dark ivory to ghost-of-ebony. They speak passionately, their thick, dark, chapped, wet, juicy lips—definitely thick, marvelously thick—lips poised for defiant and wise and provocative portraits. They are the Gay Sons of Ham, the invisible not-quite-nation of African-American gay men revealed at last and everywhere to be seen, on *Nightline,* on *A Current Affair,* on *ABC World News Tonight* and on the cover of *Newsweek.*

On *Interview*'s cover is seen yet another black face, the lean and compelling countenance of one Kenneth Gabriel, fresh from his recent triumph as the lead itinerant stud in Sam Shepard's latest Off-Broadway tale of family dysfunction and incest. With relief, you flip quickly to page 53, eager to read about at least one virile, masculine, normal black man. No doubt Gabriel will speak of his basketball-playing friendship with Eddie Murphy and detail his plans to organize a concert benefit for embattled and endangered African-American masculinity that will headline hardcore-only rap musicians and is tentatively titled *Butch Aid.* "We hope to have Mike Tyson as the host," he will say. You read, scanning for references to famous hot babes Gabriel's porked:

> *The blinds of Gabriel's sexy West Side penthouse apartment are drawn, and in the shadowy stillness of the living room I see two martini glasses sitting on an unpretentious end table. In one glass floats a half-eaten olive (reminiscent, I suddenly think, of that beauteous young light-skinned actress's body floating bum up in the pool in the opening scene of that fresh young glasses-and-goatee-wearing black director's film,* Cotton Goes to Hollywood). *In the other glass, the wet imprint of full pink lips is slowly running down the concave glassy slope. Perhaps now Gabriel, notoriously discreet about his promiscuity, will reveal the identity of at least one of his much-rumored mystery women.*

*When Gabriel finally emerges from his upstairs bed-
room, his appearance and demeanor would be an effec-
tive camouflage against the paparazzi. He wears silky
polyester Dolfin-brand aerobic-workout shorts and a
waist-length paisley print Japanese kimono which covers
the sinewed ebony chest that dazzled black and white
women in* Man of Steel.

*When he speaks, he punctuates his answers by wav-
ing a thin brown cigarette in a way reminiscent of no
one so much as Bette Davis. By the time this shocking
interview is finished, the living room is heavily layered
with a mist of blue-gray smoke.*

Q: So are you seeing anyone special? There have been so
many rumors.

GABRIEL: Why . . . no, no I'm seeing no one at all. I'm
very, very busy. With my work, you know.

Q: I know you hate to talk about these things. But I see
you have a valentine here, and there are two martini
glasses on the table. One has lipstick on it.

GABRIEL: How sloppy of me.

Q: C'mon. You can tell me.

GABRIEL: Well. If you must know—he's white.

Q: Hmmm. That'll get you in trouble with the sisters in
the community, of course. But I have a white
girlfriend myself and I think it's time we own up to
these things. Let's face it, there *are* advantages to dating white women. So why do you two keep it a secret? What does she do, what's her name?

GABRIEL: He, darling. No *s*. And I most emphatically
do *not* acknowledge *any* advantage to dating white
women.

Q: Hee Darling? Interesting. Is she an Asian model? Everyone knows how you love models.

GABRIEL: No, dear. *He,* as in him, the masculine pronoun signifying one of the male gender. Cock and balls—though of course you shouldn't print that part.

Q: And he's *white?*

GABRIEL: Yes.

Q: But what about the lipstick on the glass?

GABRIEL: My neighbor was here earlier. He wears lipstick.

Q: Sophisticated theatergoing New Yorkers will probably take this in stride, Kenneth, but not your film fans. Why come out now? Have you been threatened with an outing?

GABRIEL: No. I just thought—time to be *seen,* for real.

Q: But don't you think people will find your homosexuality shocking?

GABRIEL: My dear, in an experiment conducted by Stanley Milgram, about which every student of Nazism, the banality of evil, and the psychological history of New Haven, Connecticut, must know, *people,* as you so blandly term them—working class and white collar, university students, men and women—administered what they were *told* were increasingly painful electric shocks to a screaming, protesting actor who was pretending to be an old man with heart trouble. This they did under the flimsy pretext, offered by a man in a white laboratory coat, that electric shock was the proper way to improve the old man's memory. It was not a deviant minority that administered those shocks, but the overwhelming majority of the experiment's subjects. Most of these solid citizens, these people who retch at the suggestion that I might find their son or brother or husband attractive, turned a dial while the actor screamed through a microphone in another room. But a good many went so far as to place electrodes on the actor's wizened white body while he sat right beside them, shrieking to the living gods.

Now that, my dear, is what I call *shocking.*

Now, aren't you going to ask me about Sam Shepard? He's *divine. . . .*

("Kenneth? Kenneth?"

I turn, to see Daria's face near my own. Her black eyes are narrowed. "Kenneth, have you decided what you're gonna do?" she asks.

"You mean—?" My inner world fades, a water-reflection dissipated by a finger's touch.

"I mean are you going to try to make Hammett's sexuality an issue?"

"I, I . . ." Politics—in their raw form, like this, with words like "effectiveness" and "packaging" flying around—politics unnerve me. "I'm not sure . . . how. I mean, how to make it an *issue* per se. I mean, he wasn't, he wasn't even out, really."

"That's not unusual," Cyrus says. "In fact, that's the whole condition of most of us, Kenneth. All the more reason to do this."

"Kenneth, if you want to do it, I can give the news to the reporter covering the story at my paper as a tip. He might follow it up, call you, talk to some other people." Daria peers more closely at my face again, searching for a decision. "I'm opposed to it, but he's your cousin. You have the final say, as far as I'm concerned."

Cyrus seems to swing into view. Smoothly he says, "And if you don't want your name associated with it, Daria can tell the reporter that I said it.")

A part of me that searches for meaning in the little oddities of experience, that underlines and purports to understand irony when it appears, points out the significance of this: that so many times Cyrus has been my alter-ego, so many times I have watched him at parties glide from one gathering of people to another, bestowing laughter and light the way angels and Muses grant inspiration, or I've watched him flirt with svelte dancers and dark wet pretty boys in Speedos at poolsides without a quaver in his voice or a verbal misstep. And now, now he will say he has known and seen what I have known and seen, he will be me of his own will, this man who in fantasy has held center stage, accomplishing what I could not imagine myself accomplishing.

("Well," I begin.)

My decision seems to flicker before me like a matchflame held close to the eye.

("Well, I—"

Daria's hand rests upon my shoulder. Now, as in the past, this is her role in our friendship: to comfort, never falter, always to be present. Now I feel guilty, too. "Take some time. Think about it," she says.

"No, I—yeah. I mean, yes. Cyrus, say it's you who knows about it, and Daria, go ahead with the tip. And if it gets pushed, and they need real corroboration, I'll step forward."

"Wonderful," Cyrus says. "And I'll plan a protest."

"Oh," I say.

"What? ACT UP isn't doing a protest, are they?"

"No . . ." I say.

"Thought not."

"Well," I rise in defense, "there's the dance-riot to be planned, remember. Takes everyone's energy."

"Whatever," Cyrus answers. He can be infuriating. "But you'll be at the protest?" he asks with an exaggerated smile.

"You don't feel *pressured,* do you, Kenneth?" Daria asks, sliding her eyes over at Cyrus.

Cyrus tosses his head. "Daria, shouldn't you be at home, cooking up a mess a greens or something fuh yo man?"

Both of us laugh, relieved to turn our attention elsewhere. I am picturing Daria's man, a wiry, bearded musicology professor whose fastidiousness would likely make him blanch if he were presented with a mess of anything.

"Shouldn't you be prowling a bowling alley, tryin to *find* you a man?" Daria zings back. She tosses her head, too, and better.

"You got that from John Gielgud in *Arthur,* so don't act so pleased with yourself, missy. And I have a man."

"I guess if you call that seditty Miss TooMuchofaThang a man."

Cyrus places his hands on his hips. "Luther is not seditty. You're just feeling vengeful because I took him from you at Rena's party."

"Took him from *me?* Dear heart, he went home with you when he figured out I was too much for him!"

"Well, yes, I agree. You were rather . . . corpulent at the time.")

It is a mystical thing to watch them, and to be a part of their common laughter. Laughing with them I become a creature at once endless and as perfectly finite as a point balanced at the tip of a cone. Our laughter sweeps the world and its demands before us as if they were the merest of obstacles.

(Later—)

Time passes. I have been holding on to our laughter, grinning long after the moment and erupting again when asked to explain

(Later Daria is saying that it's time to get home.

"How's little Daria?" I ask.

"Good. Asking lots of questions. She'd like to see you again." Reproach.

"Oh, I'm sorry I haven't seen her. I'll definitely be over soon. And Professor Nkume?"

"Still keeping house?" Cyrus throws in. The professor plays househusband, though Daria has refused his proposal of marriage twice.

"Yes, bitch, he is still keeping house. And he's quite well, thank you, *Kenneth*.")

And she's off, her prickly head sinking into the grime and humidity of the subway station. We wave and continue, smiling privately. At length, Cyrus, too, is saying he needs to get back home.

("Bye!" we call at one another, and take opposite turns at the intersection.)

With a happy, contented sigh I begin to walk. Somehow unburdened now, I feel that I could dissolve upon the nocturnal breeze and become no more substantial, no less free, than a rinse of ghostly color in the glare of neon and headlights on the street.

("Kenneth."

Cyrus's voice. Small, but powerful, like the tug of a dog's choke chain.

I turn and he is just behind me. "Hmmm?"

"I forgot: I brought you a copy of the play." His cat-eye glasses flash at me like UFO signals.

"The play?" He stands, patient. "Oh! Oh, yeah, the play. Oh, I'm sorry, I was going to—!"

"Yes," Cyrus's *s* becomes a *z* here: commandant of the prisoner of war camp, smacking his riding crop into a gloved palm. "You were *going* to go by the center and pick up a copy. Does that mess run in your family? Was your mother *going* to say no to your father on the night of your conception?" He smiles now, all lips and dimples, incredibly bitchy.

And now appear his hands, which have been hidden behind his red denim shorts. He waves a one-and-a-half-inch thick packet of paper in my face.

"Script," he says.)

15

THE ADVENTURES OF EVAN MARCIALIS

Okay, it's the first time I get to pick the Game and I'm nervous.

It's almost as bad as when I got on stage the first time, senior year in high school. If I could explain it to Kenneth I would tell him about the thrill of *playing,* and the way it's mixed with fear—and shame, too, for wanting to play. How the fear and shame are really part of the thrill. Like sex would be hotter (not that I would know) if you did it in an alleyway after the clubs close, right at dawn when the delivery trucks begin to arrive. You know you could be judged, criticized, punished, and you kind of like that and hate it at the same time.

I can just see Kenneth raising that Spock eyebrow at me during the middle of a scene.

I love the Games, though. He probably thought that I

thought he was a freak when he brought up the idea, but it wasn't like that at all. It was more a release, more like permission. Like yeah, this is another something I wanted all along, another thing I was just waiting for someone to come along and *tell* me, hey, do this with me. I like playing, and not just on stage. All these serious actors, even the soap people, with all their concerns about stardom or art or both—those are concerns for me, too, but how about just playing? For its own sake.

Then of course I walk into one of these places and I feel the same guilt I felt when Daddy caught me with a bath towel on my head, shaking it like I had long hair. He didn't say anything, just—looked. Like I was taking play too seriously. That was during the '72 Olympics, so I yelled out, "I'm an Arab!" Fuckin Catholic upbringing. So I feel guilty, but the guilt gives me a little tingle.

They sure take their play seriously in here.

The carpet is plush black. Some of the lightbulbs are red, and the guy standing behind the glass counter's slick red hair and tight black T-shirt with rolled up sleeves puts him somewhere between sleaze street pimp and Dallas, Texas, young Republican. Porno prep. Guys like him only turn me on if they're walking out of or into a Holiday Inn near a highway. Once I saw a guy like that, when I was maybe thirteen, and he was with a really sleazy girl and they walked into a Holiday Inn. It made an impression on me, because I was sweating and horny and we were driving through the Southwest for our first big summer vacation and everything was exotic. I'm convinced that that's where types come from: horny adolescent minds are tabula rasas, and anything that associates itself with sex gets imprinted,

like the little ducklings who follow the first shape they see.
I like that theory.

Naturally, my first idea was games the old-fashioned
way, with whipped cream and maybe some harnesses and
leather. Ken'll want something a little more intellectual
than that.

But there *is* some great stuff in here for old-fashioned
fun: dildos by the mile, huge and small and middle-sized in
total black or Caucasian or black-man-brown or snow white,
some with little heads and some with huge heads and so
many blood vessels on them you'd be afraid a real one like
that would pop in your ass. Hand vacuum pumps to
lengthen your dick; swizzle sticks with cockheads on them;
edible body lotion—edible underwear. Then there's the
black leather hoods with scary zippers in them, and nipple
restraints (cool, but not for twenty dollars). Whips. And a
pair of stocking hose that not only covers your legs and feet,
but has a third part for a really big cock.

Porno prep is standing around pretending to arrange
dildos (what's he gonna do? rank them by size?), and he
thinks I'm smiling at him, so he grins and runs his eyes
over me. I'm not smiling at him; it's the stocking hose. I
can never get used to the idea that straight couples use this
stuff. It just seems funny to me. I mean when *I* was supposedly straight it never occurred to me. I guess that's my
Catholic upbringing again. Straight sex is supposed to be
straight: no frills and totally serious and for the Lord. That's
stupid, since their sex industry is ten times the size of ours.
But I mean, would Vicki and her boyfriend use this stuff?

She might, come to think of it. God, the way she
looked this morning. The makeup woman didn't have to do
anything with her; it's like she gets filmed in real life and

she never looks like anything but a star. And she's not like those glamour stereotypes people do when they do camp. She doesn't flash her jewels and say *dahling.* There's just an energy there—like you could get away with saying her laughter bubbles out in peals, her eyes *do* twinkle, her smile *is* radiant. And she gives so much to every scene. When we had lunch today, she had on a big shoulder-padded pastel jacket, and when she stood up from the table and her whole body came into view it was something breathtaking. And she moves—she moves and it's like watching Kenneth move, you have to watch, even though they're not the same: he's like a tiger, kind of sinister, almost. She's like a gymnast, strong but like a ballet dancer.

"Scuse me."

It's not the porno preppie, but a big brunette guy with a bodybuilder chest and nice big lips. There's a woman plastered to his arm, and for a second—Vicki?—because her hair is sort of auburn, but I see how dull it is, and how glum she is, like she doesn't want to be here or the worst thing that could happen would be that someone could tell she wanted to be here.

"How bout this, mm?" He's lovingly fingering a rubber casting of porn star Jeff Stryker's thick one.

The woman glances over at me. I step a little further back, behind them.

"Just think—about how exciting it'd be." He has no shame.

And I could almost get an erection from this. But then here comes this group of four guys laughing—laughing maybe because they're embarrassed to be in here, but anyway the rest of us act like we've been caught or something and we shut up. Even porn prep looks sheepish. These guys all have on big blue or black jeans and big black belts, and loose silk shirts that shine silver and rustle like sheets on a clothesline. They have jet-black hair, all of them, and red-brown skin like Indians in the Southwest. The straight couple kind of melts out of the way. The one who walked in first has a white cape flowing behind him. He stops in front of the glass case of dildos, a whole wall of them from foot to ceiling and corner to corner. His friends stop, too, but not gracefully like him, and they get very quiet.

He has his hands on his hips, this guy, and he's sort of beautiful. Everyone—me, the straight couple, the porno prep and the three friends—looks from him to the dildo wall, waiting.

He lets out this big sigh. "They don't have the one I want!" And then he flips back his black hair and marches out. The others run right out after him.

The porno prep gives me a what the ? look. I toss a wink at him and mouth to him at the door, *Maybe someday if I see you in a Holiday Inn.* He doesn't understand a word. What a tease I can be.

But I do have an idea.

I'm beginning to think like Kenneth, after all.

16

GAME

PLAYERS: EVAN MARCIALIS AS HIMSELF
KENNETH GABRIEL AS NICHOLAS MARCIALIS

Evan is waiting. Beyond the black bedroom door outlined by soft light (he thinks of *Close Encounters of the Third Kind,* when he looks at it), another door opens and noisily closes. Evan counts the steps taken through the foyer and then across the living room rug. He holds his breath. It is important that he be quiet and asleep

"Where the hell you been?"

"Out! I tol ya I was goin out on a date!"

"Well, get to bed! You shouldn't stay out so late!"

Evan counts more steps. The light below the door dims. His stomach is awhirl with excitement.

"Hey, kid!" The door swings open wide and a sharp beam of light arcs over the comic book–strewn bedroom floor. Evan's eyelids flutter dramatically.

"You know you ain't asleep, Ev." His hand cuffs Evan on the skull.

"I *said,* get to bed! And don't wake up your brother!"

Nicholas grunts and shuts the door again. Before his

eyes adjust he pulls off his jacket, shirt, undershirt and pants, and flings them to the floor. He stands beside the bed, his jockey shorts a beacon of white in the murky forest of brown hair covering his chest, stomach and legs. Nicholas's hands are on his hips. "Would you move the fuck over, please?"

Evan scoots over, popping open the button clasps of his pajama bottoms, which are entirely too small. Resentfully he snaps them together (he wants sexy briefs, like Nicholas has) and almost catches the fold of his foreskin in the buttons. His brother's bulky and heated presence settles into the mattress. Nicholas yanks at the covers and Evan half spins toward him.

For a while nothing is said. Suddenly Evan exhales. He can wait no longer. "So what happened?" he demands.

"What do you mean?" comes the lazy reply.

"You said you'd tell me all about your date! You said so on Sunday!" He is still at the age when a promise, if not uttered with one's fingers crossed behind one's back, is an oath sealed by God's own thumbprint.

"You read too many comics, guy," Nicholas murmurs. His broad back, clean of the fur that shrouds the rest of his body, rumbles into position directly in front of Evan's face.

"C'mon, Nicky, you said!" Evan insists. "C'mon, c'mon . . . Didya screw her?" he whispers tightly. He whines, actually.

"Did I *screw* her? Did I *sca-reww* her? What the hell kinda language is that?"

"C'mon, I'm eleven years old, don't pull that shit."

"*Shit?*" Nicholas rolls over onto his back now, depressing the small, worn mattress.

"You mean did I *fuck* her?"

Evan feels a jolt run through him. "Yeah," he hisses.

"No." And Nicholas turns his back again.

"No? But, why?"

"Why? Cause she didn't wanna, that's why. She wasn't interested. Whaddaya want me to do, call the cops? She didn't want to, that's all." Evan almost wants to cry. "I tell you, I am so fuckin sick of these girls. They never wanna do nothin, just kiss and hug and fondle. I mean, what's the big damn deal about kissin? It's nothing. Don't even get me hard. Shit. The only one who acts real is Lyntha."

"Lyntha?"

"Yeah, I told ya about her, didn't I? The one I popped that night you and Dad went to the movies coupla weeks ago?"

Evan runs his hand over the space between them on the blue sheet. "Oh, yeah."

Nicholas has now become interested in the sound of his own voice. "Yeah, I'd like to get into her shorts again. That girl knows how to rock. I'd like to bring her up here some hot night and turn on the lights so I could see everything this time. I'd have her sit on the side of the bed. Have er pull off her blouse and jiggle her boobs at me to get me a boner, and then have er put er hand down my pants, have her pull it out and stroke it for me, slow. Lean over and run her tongue up an down it and say mmmm. Then I could grab her by the back of er head with one hand and feed er my dick with the other, say, deal with my dick, baby, an give er a good hot mouthwash a cum."

"But you left me out!" Evan nearly shouts. Whines, actually.

Nicholas skips a beat before he answers. "What the

fuck do you mean, I left you out? What do you have to do with it?"

Flustered, Evan's voice climbs to a high squeak. "I wanna be in it! I wanna be a part of the story! Can't I be in it?"

His eyes fully adjusted to the darkness now, Nicholas squints over at Evan. "All right," he says—a bit whiny, to be truthful—"okay, if you have to be in it. What, you want some too?"

Evan nods, uncertainly.

"Awright, I give you sloppy seconds. Or thirds, cause I'd do her again, this time a fuck, good an hard. Kinda rough. Have Lyntha beg me for it, beg me for my big meat in her cunt. And her asshole, too. She says, take me for your pleasure, big boy, and I say, you want it, bitch? . . ."

17

EVAN AND KENNETH AT HOME

"There's another line there. I know my handwriting is scribble."

They lie together beneath crisp blue sheets on the couch bed. Kenneth is reading jumbled script by the pencil of moonlight that slices through a narrow gap in the curtains of the east window.

"I—I can't do any more of this," Kenneth says. He drops the stapled pages to the bed, where they slide down the blue slope covering his bent knee. "This—this is—I'm sorry."

Evan feels the bottom drop out of his stomach. "You don't like it?" he croaks.

"Well, I just . . . I mean, don't get me wrong, the idea, the basic idea is fine, is good . . ."

"But the execution is bad." Evan's temples are tight, tight, tight.

"I'm sorry. But I can't continue with it. It's not right. His story—I just would be more comfortable if it was, like, he's a hitchhiker and she picks him up in the desert and, you know, I don know, he eats her out" (here Kenneth grimaces, quite involuntarily) "as payment for the ride—"

"What's the matter with his story as it is?"

"It's cruel, Evan." The admission releases him enough to bring accusation to his tone. "I honestly never thought you'd come up with a Game so cruel."

Evan speaks with wicked calm. "Aren't all our Games cruel, Kenneth?"

Kenneth flinches. "Well. I guess you could say that. But . . . the cruelty is of a certain sort."

"Directed at only certain targets?" Evan says, knowing how bald is the taunt in his words. "The story is a fantasy, Kenneth. *His,* Nicholas's fantasy. Okay? And it's not like people necessarily dream the right politics. And yeah, so *your* Games have good politics, maybe, but maybe mine does too in a different way. I mean everything both of us, everything both brothers say is total pretense, total bullshit. Because they love and want each other!" He huffs, wildly and exhilaratingly wrathful.

"I think," he says at last, and licks the taste of the words off his lips, "I think carefully choosing who to be cruel to doesn't make a Game any more or less cruel."

It is in Kenneth's mind to say, *Did you rehearse that? Move your little lips over a written sentence in between posing for the television camera, did you?*—but as the subject of this discussion is cruelty, he cannot bring himself to do it.

"Maybe you're right," Kenneth says. But he doesn't believe it.

Evan says nothing.

"Maybe we can . . . come back to this, pick it up later," Kenneth says. "I'm tired now, are you? All day I've been back and forth on the phone with Daria and Cy, giving them *information*. And my father's coming. I'm tired. Could we just try it again tomorrow? I'm sorry." He pauses. His hand touches Evan's shoulder. "I love you." But this sounds whiny, he thinks.

"Your father's coming? Here?"

"Yes. To make arrangements. For the body and stuff."

Evan remains quiet for a moment, then sits up. Evidently he is unpacified. "I have something to tell you."

Kenneth looks at him.

"Member I told you I went to my old neighborhood? And I ran into an old friend?"

An old *acquaintance,* you said, Kenneth thinks, but he only nods.

"Well, we talked, and—he knew about me. About me being gay, me living with you."

"You living with me?" Kenneth sits up. "How does he even know me?"

"He doesn't. He just, I don't know, heard from someone that I'm living with a black man. That I'm sleeping with a black man."

It is odd to Kenneth to hear their relationship described this way, and out of Evan's mouth.

"And I didn't want to tell you, but he said some really stupid, offensive shit. He said—he was trying to be nice, not that that makes it better. He said he understood, because he used to fuck black whores." He leaves off, *himself.*

All at once it occurs to Evan that perhaps he has made entirely too much of absolutely nothing. So he blushes.

Kenneth, evidently, has no comment.

"And—I don't know—I just let him say those things."

Kenneth doesn't nod, doesn't frown or lift an eyebrow, doesn't move anything.

"I'm saying this," Evan continues, "because I've been thinking about this, what with the whole rape and murder thing, and it was like—I mean, I was so *afraid* or embarrassed, shamed, actually, just . . . shamed, about him knowing that I'm gay that—and this is horrible, I know, but it was just a moment, but I know it's important anyway which is why I need to discuss it with you. It was like the—the bigotry or whatever it was, was a way to unite—like this was my way out. He opened a door and I went through and that was it. It was like, this is how I get out of here with my self-esteem intact."

Kenneth should be shaking by now, with all the energy it takes to hold completely still.

"I'm confessing, but I guess I'm kinda warning you, too. About what white people will do to unite, you know? What maybe even I'm capable of doing, if I don't think."

(KENNETH WATCHES: It is impossible for me not to think the following: That every couple, every miserable unnatural grouping of human relationships into terrible *twos,* must have these moments of stumbling, stuttering confession, as if the whole population of the world were comprised of little more than variations on a single relational theme: priest and sinner. But no. In *natural* couples, in single-race couples, this moment of confession will always be about some garish instance of sexual infidelity: A has a torrid afternoon with C, who is either a creature of the most unsurpassed passion and/or beauty, or a limp, skinny thing with acne scars on his or her genitals—both equally infuriating to B, who has always suspected but could not quite bring him or herself to look at the sad, unsightly truth. But *no*. In every modern *black-white* relationship, the Negro Partner—in order to maintain the hanging-by-his-nails-at-the-edge-of-a-precipice illusion that he can wall bigotry and its effects out of the inner sanctum of his soul—will hold fast to the conviction that the one matter on which he cannot compromise is race. Ofay Partner—in order to maintain the sitting-at-the-summit-but-afraid-he-might-fall illusion that he is fundamentally a "good person" with little relation to the nasty business of oppression—will insist that race is the one matter on which there must be compromise at all costs. Hence, in this relationship, the moment of confession had to be precisely this. A white man will admit to me that he "is a racist," as if this were a matter that had never crossed my mind—and I, I will behave just as if it had not. Of course.)

"I don't want a lecture," Evan says helplessly. He is trying to be provocative.

"I can't lecture you," Kenneth says quickly. His head has now moved, and he appears to be searching for a different place to be in the room. "I can't lecture you about this. I'm not your educator. I can't lecture when it's about me."

"But it's *not* about you!" Evan is shouting. "That's the worst thing, what I'm most confessing. It wasn't you at all! You weren't even there. It was just me, Russ, and some people we were calling black. *You* weren't really there."

"I see."

"Do you want to discuss it?" It is quite possible to discern—perhaps—a timbre of glee in Evan's voice.

"It's been a long day, Evan. Good night."

If there were a bedroom door, Kenneth would have shut it—slammed it, even. As it is, he turns over and pretends to go to sleep.

Evan thinks of other things to say, all eloquent, powerful, and wounding. He does not say them. Instead he sits up for a while, the better to assess the dividends of righteous indignation. As he, too, finally turns over and affects sleep, he reflects upon the words of Annie Romano's mother from *One Day at a Time*: Never go to bed angry.

* * *

(KENNETH WATCHES: In the twilight world between waking and dream, conscious thoughts skip mischievously off their set paths to wander emancipated beneath the eaves of strange trees in hidden, subconscious groves. Tonight I come somehow to stand in a blue corridor of mirrors. They form a crooked path, but are not parallel and do not face one another. Misaligned and at mismatched angles, one mirror faces me full front, while another, placed at a ragged diagonal across the path from the first, tilts its face at me at twenty degrees. Still another on the same side as the first takes yet a different angled pose, and on and on, no two mirrors the same. I walk through, and in each reflected glimpse I see first Evan's face, then mine, then Evan's again and my own again.

Wrenched from rest by puzzlement, my eyes open to the moonlight. Awake, the surfaces of the night are black, and unreflective.

Am I always there between the mirrors, believing I see Evan when it's only me, and vice-versa?)

18

DAD'S HANDS, AND EVAN'S

KENNETH WATCHES: My father bustles. That is the word. One pictures him fussing about the kitchen of the restaurant back home, haranguing his cooks (whom he barely lets cook, probably: many were the times when Dad taught me how to fix a bicycle or change a car tire by doing it all himself and occasionally saying, "Now you see that?"— meantime I stood by holding the wrench, or whatever). His elbows don't move, forever bent at about forty-five degrees when he is in command mode, but his hands flash; more often than not his cooks, like his children, find themselves watching the palms of his hands as they sweep through the air in peremptory dismissal.

Now the funeral home owner or attendant or whoever she is leans back a bit to escape my father's hands. He handles all of this, of course. Flew out for that very purpose. Hammett's parents are too old, too sick, too afraid of airplanes, too something—some excuse for not coming and doing the job, for they did not love him.

(Dad's hands, again: I remember them tight, clutched, almost white—he's light-skinned, unlike Mother and me—as they held back his brother, Hammett's stepfather, at the Fourth of July picnic. Hammett was unjustly condemned for some minor transgression to mow the grass on the undeveloped side lot while the rest of us ate and played. Careless, angry, no doubt, he had pushed the old machine over some rocks or glass, and because inanimate objects always betray you when you feel most wronged, it spewed jagged chunks back at his face. Moaning, Hammett lumbered into the kitchen, where we were playing tonk, with a gash over his eye and on his cheek. My uncle Addison, who had been laughing and feeding my younger sister spoonfuls of gumbo, pulled rage as if from out of a hat, and set upon Hammett. Slapped him, shoved him and screamed words like *stupid* and *fucked up* and *warped.* My Aunt Raye, Hammett's mother, yelped—she could do no more, in the face of Addison's fury. Her hands flew up like ravens, speaking her fear, her reproach. In answer came my father, his big hands heaving Addison back from Hammett's hunched and sobbing form. "Now just calm down now, just calm down!" Dad said, the knuckles of his hands straining on Addison's shoulders. Addison didn't struggle. But years later, my sister and I were at a grocery store shopping for the last-minute ingredients of Mother's gumbo, and we both remembered Dad's clutching, whitish hands, and the fierce, unrepentant joy in Uncle Addison's face. It made me happy, I remember, that we both recalled the same detail, that we saw things the same way. We united over Hammett's pain, you might say.)

My father stops moving. There is a lull in the bargaining as the funeral woman looks through the pages of a three-ring binder. Naturally it occurred to no one that *I* might make the arrangements to have Hammett's body sent back for the funeral. Mother didn't so much as hint that I might help when she spoke to me on the phone. "Your Daddy'll be in New York by this evening," she warned, and went on to advise me as to how to handle him when he stopped by. "I'll let you know when the funeral is as soon as I know," she said, smooched the receiver and hung up.

She was right, of course. I could not make the arrangements. The sheer practicality of it defeats me. I have not my father's hands. (I do, however, have slightly better sense of style. It is not raining and not cold, but my father stands here gesticulating from inside a trenchcoat. No doubt the look, to him, suited the drama of the moment. One thing everyone in my family shares is a secret delight in ostentatious gestures.)

But I am here.

I lied to Evan. We were close, Hammett and I. (I knew him, Horatio.)

We were never inseparable—I spent most of my time with Daria—but Hammett and I shared something, despite the fact that our parent's quizzical glances and wrinkled-nose frowns waited at every doorway to remind us that there was something unnatural about a seventeen-year-old and a ten-year-old playing together. Mother, I think, came to know Hammett for what he was to me: a big brother, without the puffed-up manly edges, a masculine model with a softer center. A first love. I do not recall conceiving my feelings in a sexual way. I loved him because he was bigger, and male, and nice to me—a combination which, to be truthful, I have not often found since. One afternoon of that tenth

year of my life, Mother had gone out to do some of her
habitual last-minute shopping for dinner, and Hammett
dropped by. I led him, my hand in his, into the dim vault
of our basement. He followed me, patiently, through the
gloom and salty dust, with only the weak sunlight in the
upstairs living room echoing off one wall and another to
guide our way. When I had lifted the top boxes, thinking
to show him my decade-old strength (my brothers' way
had not left me unaffected) and pulled away the concealing
sheets and toys, I introduced him to Cara. Hammett smiled.
He touched her, held her in his hand. "She's real pretty," he
said. "We'll play together with her someday."

We never did. I wanted him to know her, but my pleasures, my play, I always wanted to keep to myself. But his
kindness stayed with me. He had understood better, I
thought, than Daria even, whose acrimonious relationship
with the doll came between us for a while. Afterwards
Hammett's visits were like windows and doors flying open;
they made me feel like the little kids in the beginning of
Little House on the Prairie, frolicking through green and yellow buds against a pastel blue horizon.

We were friends for many years before we had sex. But
we didn't see each other or communicate once I went to college and he left the Army. There are never good explanations
for such sunderings, and I have never bothered to fabricate
one. Perhaps I fell out of love. That's what it feels like.

It's foolish to say, but . . . his body looks different,
dead. When last I saw him, his face was not so drawn. He
was pudgier and smiled clownishly, and inside I laughed at
him. It was easy to spurn his cautious attempts to
recreate—if only in words, if I would not do more—our
one-time tryst.

That night, while Hammett rambled on, I watched him and thought of the past I refused to help him remember: it is easy (so my thoughts collected themselves) to become obsessed with or find meaning in some physical detail—in this case, Hammett's fingers. What a happy little fetish they were! I returned to them time and again to prime my secret pleasures, to smooth my passage out. But I did not perceive it—Hammett's fingers—that way. Rather they seemed to me totems of pity, emblems of the outrage of injustice. I linked them with his recurring lament about having been placed in the slow reading section of his first-grade class after failing some ludicrous standardized test on an afternoon pig-thick (my detail) with heat. "You so smart, Kenny. I wish I was like you." "But I wish I was like you!" I cried. I meant it, for a while. But the image continued to infuriate me long after I ceased idolizing him. Watching his fingers later, whenever Uncle Addison would shout at him and spray bubbles of rabid froth over his bowed head, I so wanted to caress Hammett's hands in mine, to make smooth and elegant by some magical ministration what was plain and unlovely, what had been robbed by the misanthropy of genetics of even the suggestion of articulateness, of delicacy or discernment, capability or creativity.

That was what I thought, what I crafted, when I last spoke with him. That is how I dismembered him, how I loved him and held him at a distance. I did not think then that the windows and doors he threw open for me had become padlocked portals of class and education and what we sniffingly call culture, and that when I looked back at him from my *Little House* horizon of turquoise blue, the only expression my face could manage was a smirk.

And now I see what I did not then: his hands are very much like Evan's.

"Now I expect you and Daria'll be at the funeral."

My father has bustled over. Evan, who chooses odd moments to be clever, said after meeting Dad that if he put on a hundred extra pounds and a pair of breasts, he could be a southern Italian fishwife. I picture this now, but it doesn't make me laugh. In his hands Dad is counting green bills.

"What?" I say. But of course I heard him.

"You and Daria'll be at the funeral at home!" he thunders. Since I've come out he has given me a new middle name: and Daria.

"I don't know what Daria will do. Evan and I will try to make it, but he works and there's a demonstration about Hammett's killing I want to be at." I shrug. I never follow Mother's advice about how to handle Dad.

He nods, wide-eyed, as one attempting to soothe a madman. "All right." He pats me on the shoulder. "I'm praying for y'all."

"And what would you be praying *for,* Dad?"

He shakes his head. "For your happiness, your health."

My smirk is on my face before I can edit it. But he doesn't notice.

"Next thing is to go light a fire under these damn *cops!*" he says. The contemplation of this skews the handsome features of his face. Whatever Evan says, he is still very good-looking, my father.

He looks at his watch. "Well, it's after five. Let's go eat, honey."

We walk out together and go to dinner.

Today I inhabit hands, and fingers.

19

THE MOVEMENT

KENNETH WATCHES: Children need their fathers. This is the lesson for the morning, endlessly and nauseatingly repeated. *Children need their fathers.* He never shuts up—Alton Willis, one of Cyrus's cronies, a marvelously beautiful man whose mouth ruins everything. He is fighting for custody of his son (the one variation to this mantra is, *Sons need their fathers,* which, in view of my paternal progenitor's recent visit, I simply cannot stomach), he tells us while kneeling his marvelous body over white posterboard on the floor. His ex-wife has turned vengefully to the Catholic Church since she found herself in sexual competition with penises and is determined to shelter her child from a life of perversion and sin. (Alton is of the view that were she African Methodist Episcopalian, his troubles would be over; I am more skeptical.) We—all eight of us here, in a chilly room at the Lesbian and Gay Community Center—learn much about Alton that we have no wish to know. Once again he bursts into a harangue about his ex-wife, and Sylvester and I share a look that says something like: the kid's better off with the Marquis de Sade than with Alton. Actually this is a relief, as irritation with Alton is the one thing Sylvester and I have ever shared. We are both black, gay, actors, and unemployed. But he is, or seems to be, firmly ensconced in a network of fabulous friends and fellow artistes, and I am not. I have a white lover, and he (vociferously) does not. So, after rolling our eyes at Alton and to one another, we look away.

I wish Cyrus would hurry back. The overcast gray of the summer sky is enough to depress me.

("The protest starts at ten," I said before I walked out of the door. "I'll see if I can get there," Evan said, and stumbled into the bathroom with one eye closed and his red briefs slung unevenly across his white buttocks.)

I have butterflies in my stomach.

Now Cyrus arrives, to widespread (or so it seems to me) relief. "I *found* our tardy ones," he sneers cheerfully. Some ten or so men, and three women, crowd restlessly behind him. "They act like they can't find their way around outside Fort Green and Park Slope."

"I wasn't born in this damn town" / "I knew where it was but none of these niggas would listen" / "Girl, you didn't know nothin" / "Don't pay attention, Cy just likes to instigate, *right,* Cy?"

There is a cacophony. Instructions, mostly from Cyrus, are given, slogans swiftly etched, signs collected, chants suggested, discarded, revised and rehearsed. The room grows humid with the proximity of bodies. I find myself sitting on the floor, slightly apart from a coterie of four, one of whom, the nearest—handsome but nothing special—occasionally looks and flashes a magnetic smile, even offers some jaunty comment to which I cannot think of any appropriate response except my own, undoubtedly far less lustrous, grin.

Cyrus rises, dapper in black, to inform us just once more that this is a simple protest: we will block traffic on a street near where *it* happened, perhaps for an hour; Jewella and Ray are veterans of this kind of thing, and along with Cyrus will serve as marshals, dealing with the police and any other foreseeable obstacles. "If everything goes okay, we should maybe end with a short march," Sylvester volunteers. Cyrus, who does not enjoy being upstaged, frowns—which opens an altogether new discussion.

At some point we're walking over there.

Cyrus has come by at intervals to touch me and ask how I'm doing, and now drops back from the front of the group to do it again. On his way he squeezes shoulders and doles out unsolicited (but witty, of course) advice with a campaigning politician's energy.

"Do you know what *movement*—a movement—feels like, Kenneth?"

Oh, God.

"My mother told me about how when she was just a freshman in college in Louisiana, about 1960, 1961, some students got arrested for sitting at a whites-only lunch counter in Baton Rouge. Rumors started flying around about a march through downtown. Organizers, people who'd helped start marches and protests all over the South, were there to help, and everyone was talking about it. My mother's roommate's parents called her and told her that she'd better not march or they'd take her out of school. She convinced my mother to go to the church where the marchers were getting organized anyway. When they got to the church, it was packed. Everyone they knew was there, and everyone was nervous and excited. The organizers were giving instructions when a man from the campus administration arrived and told the students to sit tight and not do anything. He threatened to expel the students who marched, and when some folks yelled out that all the students were there, he said they'd close the school down. People got scared. My mother wanted to leave. Then somebody got up in the church and pushed him aside. He said, 'We gon march! I don't care what these crackas or niggas say about it, those boys are in jail for alla us and we gon march!' And Mama said there was a rush inside of her, inside everybody, and she and her roommate and almost everyone just got up, got up out of the pews and *moved*. They moved because they had to, because they *got* moved. They went out there and marched. Mama said that as far back and in front as you could see there was nothing but black folks, quiet and dressed in their Sunday-go-to-meeting clothes."

His face is bright, eyes keen. All of his features seem sharper. "What happened?" I ask.

"The police came after some people with tear gas, and there were apparently altercations, but my mother wasn't part of the group who got arrested. The campus administration closed down the school and sent everyone home, and didn't reopen for about a month. Mama didn't go back when it did. She joined SNCC, and then ended up on the Freedom Rides throughout the South. She told me she couldn't stop moving once she started. That's how it feels, sometimes, in a movement like that, one that's new and powerful. You feel swept up."

He hugs me tight, shoulder-to-shoulder, and then is off.

I suppose he is likening all this to our "movement" today, but if so, I cannot share his optimism. We are but seventeen people, several with "plans" ("I have to leave at ten forty-five latest," at least two have said, and Alton needs to pick up his car before the mechanic leaves for Fire Island); *The Daily News* buried Cyrus's tip about Hammett's sexual practices somewhere in paragraph eleven of twelve on a page 20 story, and though the Reverend Sharpton's people have made inquiries into the matter, nothing seems to be happening. And like Cyrus's mother, I'm scared.

As the sun burns off the morning haze, I am shivering. A black man, older, wearing a baseball cap, drives by in a long relic of a car and I quail, knowing that he knows *us*, instantly.

Mind games, I tell myself, to steady my wobbling Weeble nerves.

Well, at least today Cyrus has given me something different. Today he didn't preach that tawdry gospel of the Self, of Identity and Will, but rather gave me another vision. *Swept up.* I like the sound of that. I'll be swept up one day, God willing.

It's a feeling I wish that I had now. Instead I am dizzy and disjointed, as if this circle we tread and retread waving signs and chanting were a spinning carnival ride. I chant, but there is no power to it; already I imagine I may be hoarse. I gaze straight ahead, face set and determined, but I do not dare look long or directly at the modest but consistent number of faces which come to watch. Glances confirm my fears (they would, wouldn't they?): I see hostility, indifference, incomprehension. The black faces unsettle me most: silent, grim, neither supportive nor reproachful, they stand immobile, sentinels rather than witnesses—and I have the sense that it is not our safety or the sanctity of our cause that they are guarding.

I want to scream at them. How can this be, that you can stand there looking that way, shaking your heads that way? How is it that what we are makes us no longer a part of you? We cannot be ascribed to the sinister influence of outside forces—we are no more or less a product of the white man than you—and there can be no claim that lunar dust sprinkled our mothers' wombs to freakish effect before birth, no appeal to Freudian failure that can save you from claiming us as your own. We are you, as you are us. How then did we lose you?

My rage cowers behind a stone face. And it withers, with despair or hope, I cannot say, when I begin to think that some of the very people who marched with Cyrus's mother could be standing here behind these undifferentiated scowls.

I look for diversions from my paranoia: the police provide a small one, but not for long. They, too, watch closely and direct the moderate Saturday morning traffic around us without much incident, though the drivers, more irate than anyone, howl their fury with noisy horns. Some ACT UP folks, two of them plus two others I don't recognize, happen by, stop, look, see me and flash a thumbs-up. But they are evidently going someplace else.

I am about to become even more cynical about this "protest"—what's the risk, really, with the protection of police who are no more ferocious than the neighborhood alley cat, and with the only emotions raised those of people who resent slower traffic? I think this as bravado, of course.

Merely to bear a look askance is to me like standing before the charge of unleashed hounds and firehoses.

And now God answers my bravado in the form of a thirtyish black man with a round mini-'fro and lean body. Squirrelly and tense, he darts two steps out of the crowd of onlookers just as Cyrus passes him. For a horrid instant those of us who see him fear—and know we cannot prevent—violence.

But the man does nothing more frightening than insistently tap Cyrus's shoulder. "So, so what?" he fires, like a man not quite able to restrain himself. "You saying the man who got killed here was a homosexual?"

"Yes, he was," Cyrus calmly replies after a small recoil. "He was and we think it should be called attention to, that he was a black gay man who was raped."

"Why you wanna say that about the man? Did you know him? You probably don't even know him! How this gon help anything?!" His outrage flares and again nearly pulls me from the circle to Cyrus's rescue. But Ray is headed over there. The man sees him, and his eyes skim past us and come to rest on the two watching policemen.

"You wrong! This is wrong!" he sputters, jabbing a finger at Cyrus. Then he turns and quickly plows his way through the small crowd.

"I'd love to discuss it with you further!" Cyrus calls, but he must be relieved. Some of the onlookers laugh, and Cyrus, always a ham, bows.

"I think I recognized that man," Bithia, who is in front of me, says to Gayle, who's in front of her. "Remember when we got burglarized and went to report it, the clerk who we waited in that long line to talk to and he said we had to call first, and you got in an argument with him?"

"Oh, yeah," Gayle says, and turns her head to look at him again. But he is gone. "Hall, Hill, something like that? I never did file that complaint against him."

Today I inhabit someone who seems to belong to everyone but me.

20

THE ADVENTURES OF EVAN MARCIALIS

This is exactly the kind of shit that always happens to me. No wonder I can never keep my thoughts, my feelings, anything, straight. I'm way late. First it takes me like a whole half hour to decide I'm even gonna show up, because I'm still mad at him and he knows it, but I'm also feeling completely guilty because of the whole thing with Russ, and then all the horrible shit he's going through about his cousin. Does he know I'm worried about him? Probably not. He never knows what I go through because of what he goes through, and then he doesn't know I go through anything, period. Or maybe he does. I don't know.

Shit. And then Allan calls up, totally out of nowhere, and I'm like, Christ, I'm fired. But then he tells me how pleased everybody's been with my work, that I've suddenly clicked and they're talking about expanding my storyline.

Especially, he says, the chemistry with Vicki. And then the axe: "You and Vicki are doing so well together, in fact, that we'll certainly make you the new hot couple. And, just a word of advice—only a suggestion, no pressure—if anything's *possible* there, I'd urge you and her to go out publicly together. Make it kind of a thing. It would give us publicity and be good for the ratings, we think—and you know how much help we need there."

Make it kind of a *thing*! Just a *suggestion,* if anything's *possible*! What a fucker. Completely untrustworthy. He probably came up with this idea himself and told Phyllis and Edwin and everyone that Vicki and me'd be up for it. I mean, he knows I'm queer. Just a *suggestion.* Like: Clean up your image, you flaming fag, and help the show at the same time. Fuck. I wonder what Vicki thinks. I mean, we are pretty close. In another life, maybe, we could have been lovers . . . I don't know. I don't know what the fuck I'm supposed to do.

I gotta be near the place now. I hear chanting. Can't make it out, though. Yeah, this is it. I see the signs: WE WON'T DIE IN SILENCE. HAMMETT WADE WAS A BLACK GAY MAN; WHY DON'T YOU KNOW THE WHOLE STORY? BLACK AND GAY: DON'T DIVIDE US IN HALF. OUT OF THE CLOSET AND INTO THE STREETS.

There are more people here than I thought there'd be. Cops and traffic. It's like a little circus. And one of those guys is major cute. . . .

Ken doesn't see me yet. I wonder if he saved me a sign or if there's even room for me. It would be stupid for one white guy to walk around just yelling.

SUPPORT GAY PEOPLE OF COLOR.

This woman bumps into me. "Oh, I'm sorry," I say.

"Garth?"

Oh, shit.

"Garth *Gaines*! You're Garth Gaines! Kelly, it's Garth from *Lovelife*! Oh my God would you sign me I mean my autograph?"

Oh, my God. I start signing my name before I even know what I'm doing. And now *everyone's* saying: Oh, my God. Ten girls touching me, pens and napkins and paper waving at my face. They're clogging the sidewalk and people are staring. Something tells me to smile and I do. "I think you're *hot*," one girl says. Her face is gone immediately. "My name is Inji. I-N-J-I!" Somebody grabs my butt, I swear. "You're *so* good." "Don't *push* him, you guys!" How many of them are there? I see this tall black woman, looking at me over the others' heads. She has a dark face and an amazing smile. Past her, I see Cyrus, looking over this way while he marches.

"Keep up the good work, Garth," the black woman says, loud but dignified, sounding really cool, and then she leaves.

"Do you *live* around here?" someone asks. I'm signing another person's hand. "Where'd you go?" "Just over there, across the street. Some gay thing, except they're all black. Who's *he*?"

I can't stay here. This isn't going to end. I see more people headed over here who were watching the demonstration, and these girls, some of them, they look, like, hungry. I just have to leave.

I push back after this last autograph, say I'm late, smile like a Charlie's Angel, and run like hell.

21

EVAN AND KENNETH AT HOME

They stand facing one another, Evan's mouth full of blue foam and crammed with a toothbrush, Kenneth sweating and silent. It is after midnight.

"Oh, hi!" Evan speaks through the toothpaste.

"Hi." Kenneth says. He seems to stare.

Evan wipes his mouth with the back of his hand. "Did you get my note?"

"No. I haven't been home. Did you get my messages?"

"No! I just walked in. I haven't even checked the machine yet."

"Oh." Kenneth shrugs, pulls his left elbow into his stomach with his right hand. "Well, I just left a couple messages telling you where we were. When you left the demonstration—!"

"You *saw* me?" The pink inside of Evan's mouth is overlaid with a light blue sheen. "God, Kenneth, there was a—!"

"A mob scene, I know." Kenneth nods. "I didn't actually see you, but Cyrus did and he told me. He said it looked crazy."

"Nothing like that's ever happened to me. I mean, I wasn't afraid, but it was bizarre. I didn't know what to do. I thought they'd never stop, so I figured I had to leave."

"You're becoming famous." Kenneth smiles. Now he moves around Evan and toward the kitchen. "We waited a little bit after the people started leaving, but then I figured you weren't coming back."

Evan follows Kenneth to the refrigerator door. "I just didn't know what to do. I came home and waited for you to call. I waited around and then Vicki called because there's this weird scene we're doing with another guy—Brett, I told you about him—and she invited us to come to her place and rehearse. So when I didn't hear from you . . ."

"Yeah, it took forever to return all the stuff," Kenneth says as he breaks ice from a plastic tray and places a few cubes into his glass. "Then Cyrus wanted to go to lunch with a bunch of us. I called you from the restaurant, but I guess you'd left by then."

"I'm so sorry I wasn't there," Evan says plaintively. Kenneth shakes his head as if to dismiss the matter. "How'd it go? From what I saw there seemed to be a lot of people."

"You think so? I guess. Cyrus was really pleased. I don't know. It doesn't help Hammett in any way, which I guess maybe I had some stupid hope that it might. And I'm not sure it helps anything else, either. What has demonstrating ever done since, like, 1978?" He drinks deeply from the glass, his Adam's apple traveling down his outstretched throat.

(KENNETH WATCHES: The peculiar thing—it flies
at me as I shrug, as if Hammett and justice and
rights and all that didn't matter, when nothing
could be further from the truth—the peculiar
thing is that Evan, revered, loved, sometimes
worshiped, recedes now into irrelevancy. The fate
of the good white liberal, maybe: to fade, when
comes the violent, illiberal moment his existence
lulls us into believing will not occur. Maybe.)

Now Kenneth goes to the couch bed, which has already been folded out. He sits heavily on its edge. Compul-
sively he mumbles toward the bathroom, "So you rehearsed
all night?"

"Uh huh. Well, we had dinner, too."

"Oh. Well . . . do you think you'll be able to partici-
pate in the dance-riot thing, the demonstration?"

"The—? Oh! When is it?"

"Couple of weeks from now. Early on a Tuesday morning, I think."

"Yeah, sure. I mean, if I don't have to tape anything."

They don't say anything else.

Finally Evan's tall naked form appears in the bathroom
doorway.

"Ken?"

"Mmhm?"

"How are you feeling?"

"Fine." Evan sees that Kenneth's clothes are wadded
on the floor beside his half of the bed.

"I'm so tired," Kenneth says—rather aggressively,
Evan thinks. "I'll be more energetic tomorrow. Promise."
His eyes are solidly closed.

The light goes out and Evan climbs into bed beside Kenneth. He lays a hand on Kenneth's shoulder. "Okay," he says, and goes to bed knowing that he's not horny but disappointed that they are not having sex anyway.

22

BEWITCHED

KENNETH WATCHES: It is cold. The weather—the weather; can we even speak of it as one entity?—the weather, pulled taut by the excesses of man's inhumanity to earth and air, now snaps back and forth: too hot, then cold, always unseasonable. There is a chill out there, November visiting August, Pilgrim's Winter we might call it, and that rain is no good spring thing held over to clean out the streets, but a nasty, hellish wrath. Were I to hold a bird captive in my open palm outside the window, the poor creature would melt, become warped gray bones and molted blue feathers, and my exposed arm would turn a shade of purple.

So I sit inside, watching a miserable episode of miserable *Bewitched*. Today I hate it. I hate Darrin, male chauvinist sexist pig extraordinaire that he is, especially the second one. Such a bigoted little man, and ugly. Samantha, as always too accommodating, has procured for him an amulet that will make her mother Endora behave nicely to him.

Endora and Darrin are in the kitchen now, and Darrin, typ-
ically for his stripe of worm, is taking advantage of the situation to command Endora to make him a sandwich. But,
fool, he does not have the amulet. "Make it yourself,
Derwood," Endora snarls, long arm stretched above her
head, the side of her body pressed against the refrigerator.
"Make it, and choke on it."

Derwood. How I hate him. I see him now, daughter
Tabitha grown and off in California somewhere producing a
TV news show, son Adam away at college, Samantha no
longer fending off the relatives because they've stopped
coming around, but taking trips to Brazil and Indonesia
by herself over Darrin's objections, not using her powers
because she's afraid of them, is ashamed of them finally,
the way Darrin wanted it. Darrin's head of McMann &
Tate now—Larry kicked it in '80, vigorously celebrating
Reagan's election on top of a cheap prostitute—and the
agency mostly does political ads for the Republicans and
beer commercials: Darrin's handiwork is always full of
blonds with even teeth and rippling American flags.

But suppose something different. It was Christmas-
time, say—better, the Fourth of July—and Adam had been
in east Africa since January for his semester abroad, and Mr.
and Mrs. Stephens were preparing for the homecoming,
Samantha in the kitchen mixing up the potato salad and
basting the ribs for the grill, Darrin in the den twiddling
with new pearl-handled golf clubs. And suppose the door-
bell rang, and the Stephenses ran to the door, golf club and
mixing bowl respectively in one hand, and the other hand
fumbling over its spouse in competition to slide back the
dead bolt and twist the knob when—*wham!* The door flew
open. And there was Adam—recognizably Adam in his face,

but Adam with thick lips, burnished black skin, and a space
between his teeth. Adam with thick and kinky and long
and ropy hair, Adam walking through the front door with
an old man's grace and wisdom in his stride, a young boy's
spring in his step. Adam walking in with a spear, maybe.

"SAAAM!!" You can hear Darrin scream, his face red
and contorted, his little no-lips trembling like the golf club
in his shaking hand. Turns out that Adam, using spells and
ceremonies Grandmama Endora had taught him on the sly,
had communed with his roots in Africa—his true roots, the
roots of humankind. And communing thus, on the veldt
say, at the feet of the Mountains of the Moon, in a deep
cave, he awakened She-Who-Was-in-the-Beginning, the
Spirit the first humans worshiped when they knelt down in
the grass to make their sacrifices and bless the hunt and the
gather. Suppose it was She who marked him as her own and
sent him back endowed with a life's mission:

"Grandma Endora, Her High Priestess, is going to send
me back into the past to make a New Covenant With the
Land," suppose Adam said while his parents stared open-
mouthed in horror, potato salad-to-be and golf club limp
upon the carpet. "We're gonna return to the Mother Goddess,
to the Old Ways. We're gonna fuck whoever we want to"
(read "fuck" here as happily vigorous and entirely mutual, as
a shock word in the Stephens household, totem of the New
Dis-order, not as a semi-violent act of macho self-definition)
"and whoever wants us. We're gonna fuck in your bed,
Daddy. And we're gonna do it in the name of God(dess)."

Yes. Yes, suppose that. And suppose Endora arrived
then in a nimbus of cloud and fire, bringing Uncle Arthur,
cousin Serena, punk vampires, Edwardian fairies, renegade
cherubs, sorcerers and santeros out of Spanish Harlem,

houngans and vadoun priestesses from Haiti, hoodoo root doctors from old New Orleans, West African elves, and a fallen seraph who had been exiled to the Amazon. Suppose that. And suppose they did a big dance, the Ghost Dance, led by a Plains Indian shaman and a south Texas bruja, and they did it in the living room, with Darrin at the center, trapped on the coffee table, while Samantha stood off in a corner, trying not to giggle.

"Oh, and with what *power* I shall destroy them!" Adam exulted, and he lifted his father's chin as feudal lords (we might suppose) lifted the chins of village girls brought into the castle to spread out on his sheets. "With hatred—a hatred five hundred years old, subtle, fine, hard and relentless, a hatred surviving unchanged like the cockroach, the shark. *Give us back our land!* they tell me. *Let our peoples go!* And so it shall be. Mother wants her children to dance again."

(Ah, this is lovely. I can taste this.)

Suppose then that they bound Darrin hand, foot and (most importantly) mouth—Uncle Arthur did it with a flip of his palm in the air, like a vertical backhand slap—and dragged him into Endora's spell, as she sent them, son and father, in a puff of smoke and an elegant pass of wrinkled fingers, into the Past, into the time of Obscenity: the Old South. Maybe they arrived on the doorstep of Tara, and Adam cowed Rhett, et al. with a flash of lightning; maybe they interrupted the nigger fights out in the Mississippi backwoods of Faulkner's Sutpen's Hundred, and Adam choked the life out of Sutpen with a braid of his hair, as an afterthought, as casual, vengeful excess.

And then they climbed a tall hill, waded through dusty, hot cottonfields to get to the base, Adam in a long flowing robe of off-white against the sleek black of his African hue,

Darrin all bundled up like a papoose, floating along in midair with only his bugged-out, fearful eyes showing him to be a man, not a demon. And scores of slaves—the "wild" men of Sutpen's Hundred throwing off their animal countenances to dance with the joy of men who were never enslaved, the Butterfly McQueens of Tara not birthin no babies no more and not caring neither and maybe tossing a few of those master race chillun from a high window in the Big House just for sport—following along behind, Cecil B. DeMille style. Their jubilant chant rose, their angry, ominous hum almost as crazed as the sound of *Heil!* in the stadium at Nurnberg. The sound of doom. Doom, thundering like a running herd of horses' hooves over the plains. *Doom.* Thundering over the cowering old men, the women and children, the crackers gathering upon their horses to assail the foe—guilty victims all, struck dumb at the coming of doom.

And on that hill, the Center—or maybe not the Center, not the head, but the heel, the Achilles Heel—of a history and civilization built upon bigotry. On its summit Adam stood tall and revelled in the feel of it, in the knowledge that this was the tortured boy of the Mother, a cancerous polyp hill of hate and greed and murder.

From his robe (who knew from whence it came, where 'twas hidden? in his flesh perhaps he carried it, like the barbed wire worn by saints beneath their tunics) he drew a cross the length of a man's forearm, made of oak and adorned with a coil of ivy.

He held it aloft.

"This is for Her Children, our brethren who starved in the bowels of the ships and were cast as carrion to the sharks during the Middle Passage; for broken men, swinging like puppets from the limbs of trees in a land they had fought on foreign shores to save; for mothers, beaten by men who wield their penises as weapons, abandoned by children who embrace instead narcotic frenzy; for a people failed by hope, by government, by God! This cross is for us."

And as he plunged the cross into the red earth of the hill the ground shook, and a fierce wind, keen as a scimitar's sweep, whistled out of the sky.

"This," he cried, drawing another cross from his robe, "is for Her Children, our brethren who welcomed bearded strangers to their shores and were paid with slavery in ore mines; for those who were paid with the indignity of offering their bloodied backs as cushions for their captors' rape of young girls; for those who were paid with promises that proved grass does not grow nor wind blow! This cross is for us."

He spiked it into the red earth, and the ground shuddered. A fierce hail of white lightning rained down from the stormy sky.

"And this," Adam cried, drawing a last cross from his robe, "is for Her Children, our brethren, for all who in the spite of the Father and his minions were stripped of their names, of their loves and lusts and histories, and who labored and suffered and died to reclaim them! This cross is for us."

. . . And then suppose: Nothing.

Silence.

In the shade of a tall oak on a flat green plain, a black man in an off-white robe stood, and beside him knelt a white man cloaked in black—once his father—whose eyes sagged in red-rimmed half-circles slick with moisture, blinking.

"Good," said Adam, patting the man who had been his father on the head. "Look. It's different now."

Now *that* would be a fun episode.

Today, I inhabit the Dream.

23

They lie together on the couch bed in the livingroom
bedroomdiningroom. Evan thinks he might want to talk—
about something, he's not certain what. Kenneth has
other ideas.

"Please."

"No. It's not safe."

"Please?"

"It's not *safe.*"

"Oh, *please,* Evanitch. It's as safe as anything else. You
didn't have any problem last time."

"Yeah, but then you did it, and I still haven't gotten
around to being tested. . . ."

"You're making excuses, Evanitch. Now pull out your
fucking dick and do what I tell you."

"Ha ha."

"You're getting hard."

"I am not."

"Yes, you are."

"Okay, maybe a little. You know how you talking dirty works me."

"So you'll fuck me?"

Evan sighs deeply. "I guess."

"Who am I?"

"You," Kenneth answers. He wonders if he is lying. "Just you." Repeating makes it so, maybe.

"What am I?" Evan is confused.

"Just a man." Kenneth's tone is almost one of lament. "Only a man."

". . . Is it on?"

"Mmmhmm." His erection is really rather strong, reluctance or no.

"Good."

"Okay, so how do you . . . ?"

"No, not that way . . . Yeah. Oh!! Yeah. That's better. Like that."

"God, you're so . . . I better just go slow. . . . Why are you laughing?"

"Nothing, nothing. Really. Just . . ."

"Am I—?"

"Yyyes. Oh. Oh. Yes, you are."

(KENNETH WATCHES: Now. Now, see how it . . . *You like white dick, boy? Yeah, you want it. You like it. Get down there. Hold him down! Yeah, black bitch, I'm gonna give you just what I gave her.* I hate you I like it I hate you I hate you I like it I likes it not I hate it I hates you not I hate)

"Are you okay? You . . ."

"You— No! I—!"

"Kenneth?"

(KENNETH WATCHES: Stop. Stop. He's gentle. He's not)

"Are you all right? I'll stop."

(KENNETH WATCHES: *Some big white dick, huh, boy? Big as y'all's, huh? Jack off in his ear, Jack, while I split his ass open. . . .* No. Like Cyrus said? He's just one white man)

"Ken?!"

"Yeah. Yeah, Evan. I'm fine. . . . You don't have to . . ."

"You sure, because—!"

"Yes. I'm fine."

Kenneth opens his eyes, looks up. A stripe of light through the window blinds crosses his wet cheek.

"Fuck me harder," he says.

And in between geysered gasps, his words, like a metronome, until they both come:

"That's it. That's it."

(KENNETH WATCHES: Tonight, Evan inhabits me.)

PART THREE

AFTERWARDS...

24

CAN'T HELP LOVIN THAT MAN OF MINE

KENNETH WATCHES: This morning in Kansas City, Kansas (there is such a place, though the megalomaniacal Missourians would have the world believe otherwise), Hammett's funeral is being held. New York City, New York, commemorates the event with appropriately overcast skies, against which its towers—its World Trade, its Pan American, its Empire State—stand revealed as the dim monuments to lifelessness they are.

I could not be there with him. Mother would have wanted me to give the eulogy. She alone among my family is impressed that I'm an actor and believes that I should be on display at every opportunity. Whenever I'm at home, a video camera is appended to her shoulder. It's her dream, I think, to have a video collage of all of her children, a documentary of snazzy black-and-white images of our faces, with music by Nina Simone and Aretha Franklin in the background. And she's serious about her dreams; a few weeks ago she told me that she's begun night classes in film and video production at a local community college. My sister laughs at this, not unsympathetically. My brothers roll their eyes, but then cannot restrain the ham that lives in all the Gabriel family, and so strike bold poses while reaching for the TV remote control and opening the refrigerator door.

I wonder at my mother's desire to collect images like beasts in a menagerie. It's something that seems to travel down the bloodline.

But I could not be there with him. My eulogy would not have been what they wished to hear. It would have baffled them, perhaps incensed them. And I don't know anyway whether I would have had the words to say good-bye. Good-bye, like I love you or I hate you, I lock away in a little box for private examination. When I speak the words to others they are only copies, stilted burlesques of the feelings they are meant to communicate.

So I couldn't be there.

No doubt Dad is giving the eulogy even now; he will be sagacious and pious and eloquent and endearingly sincere. He will not tell the mourners, who live a thousand miles away and cannot be expected to do anything about it anyway, that the police investigation has stalled—if indeed it could be said that it was ever moving at a speed that would make the state of being stalled something to comment upon. He will not and need not tell them that, between him, me, Mother, Aunt Raye and Daria, we have managed probably twenty shouting, cursing altercations with the NYPD detectives, demanding action, all to little avail. He will certainly not repeat what the police continue to repeat: that the prostitute who was raped has so far been unable to produce a coherent or consistent identification of her attackers. "She hasn't been right since it happened," the detective I spoke to said, "and many of these women have a drug history, you know," he added very knowingly, very confidentially. Or that the police say no one seems to have seen much of anything that they can remember, not the other prostitutes she knew, not nosy late-night corner store cashiers, no one. Dad will not mention that Daria, when she has an infrequent free moment, has put her journalistic skills to work in seeking information, with no useful result; and that I have given a very impassioned account of the incident at a Monday night ACT UP meeting, for which I received much sincere sympathy but little practical help or advice.

Dad won't say any of this. He will be soothing. He will talk about death and life, and make them both things of wonder and magic and deep meaning, things that no one need fear. Mourn, yes, he'll say, but do not, do not ever despair.

Meantime I sit here upon a park bench. For me there is no audience, no grieving congregation crying out its approval of my sorrow and sharing my loss, no room packed with angry activists roaring that my fury is their fury. I am—and let's laugh at the melodrama, let's roll our collective eyes heavenward and sigh that we are so very bored with Kenneth Gabriel and his incessant complaints—*I* am alone.

But look: like the cavalry, a man comes. I have been watching him from afar as he approaches slowly from the south, a woman beside him. She talks intensely. *He* is per-

fect. This man—we must speak the title with reverence, as
a hallowed name might be whispered in a grotto in the Pal-
estinian desert, for there is all about him the potent aura
that we ascribe to the one true deity of the modern world,
the paragon Male. It is in his stride—easy, powerful, King
of the Jungle cliché—and in his musculature, and in (this
most of all) the slightly indulgent smile of his tensionless
mouth turned down to the woman. In the jut of his goatee
we divine pride, the disposition of a warrior, a leader; we see
a forward look, aimed at the Revolution. Mustache and
thick dark curving eyebrows. What satanic good looks, ripe
for objectification, for the eroticism of worship.

And oh, yes, he is what we worship, all of us, and it
is curled there, into a strutting, preening lump, coiled at
the bottom of his zipper. Someone somewhere in ancient
times saw the thing and thought there was something compelling, something magical about it. Another man, no question; only a man could become so enamored of such a thing.
He got down and worshiped it, saw it in his dreams, and
carved and painted and erected buildings that reminded
him of that thing. Dick brain. And now here we have the
worshiped being incarnate, in the skin of what is most
feared and most hated and most (what? envied? desired?): a
black man.

In locker rooms over the years, white boys have sat and
will sit upon benches and stare, enthralled by His glory.
"You're all muscle." "You don't have an inch of fat on your
body." "You're really built; do you work out a lot or is it
natural?" "How much do you bench press?" These are the
heterosexuals. (The gay ones, terrified if they know themselves at all, say nothing.) They move, tentatively but without deviation, to ingratiate themselves. Amicably they share

with Him insights on the prospects of the local football/
basketball team (he runs track, but that's of no consequence). They make some appreciative but passing reference
to the sexiness of a popular woman of color (she is not the
woman here, in the park, who wears a short afro and is
black, black, black; she was the copper-colored one with
flat, pressed hair who sang "Evergreen" at the school talent
show). They remark, casually, that they play their Public
Enemy collection loudly even though Mom detests it.
Elated they then extol to others His high virtues, proclaim
passionately that He is the "coolest." This ostentatious en-
thusiasm they reserve only for Him. With Him, such brief
conversations are intimacy; they are conquests to be treasured and flaunted before one's fellows.

But this is only our first look, the shocked and ensor-
celled gaze when we see Him finally as we have always
wished to: naked, sweating with some athletic exertion, or
clean and buffed and shiny after his shower, a Greek god-
shape clothed in skin like purple velvet or black silk. This
image we cannot forget: to behold it is what child psychol-
ogists might call witnessing the Primal Scene. Years later,
of course, his visage comes to arouse not adulation but terror, not choked and hopeless lust but scorn and pity. En-
grossed in the numbers crowding our ledgers and stock
portfolios we glance up and see him; he has stolen into our
offices and we are fumbling with the telephone for building
security's emergency number, but his face is so imploring
even as it holds itself rigid in pride, so full of *potential* even
beneath the smut and stench of failure and decline. We give
him a job. He needs it. He sweeps, lifts, totes—or perhaps
sells on the floor, but only under the watchful eye of our
big-bellied manager, who years before would not have been

fit to lick His smelly little toe, and we could not have
imagined then such a sorry turn of events as this because
He would have been a professional ballplayer (He ran track,
we dimly recall, but that's of no consequence), He would
have filmed commercials and after retirement opened a restaurant (at which we would be special customers with our
own table, naturally), and isn't it all a shame and a waste.
We fire him, of course. He does not work out. Not so much
the quality of his work, which, while rough-edged, to be
sure, certainly was satisfactory (though later even this rudi-
mentary work ethic crumbled), but his attitude: so pro-
foundly *ungrateful,* curt, belligerent. Moody. Uppity. And he
would never warn us when his mood had changed, never explain what had happened to him at home (broken family,
domineering wife, drug-crazed children, the usual) or on the
streets to set him on edge. We asked. He would not answer.
Finally he laid that final straw upon backs—which had so
willingly taken on his burdens!—he screwed up an order,
spoke testily to a customer who complained, allowed the
garbage to pile up for the ninety-ninth time, *something,* and
we let him go, had to, and what a shame and waste it is,
too. Someone else gave him a job later, but as we knew he
would, he failed that, as well, and now he stalks the streets
like a wild man, sometimes quietly begging, other times
shouting, demanding, clutching. Recently he was arrested
and then released, and we have begun to warn our daugh-
ters never to speak to him, to cross the street rather than
share a sidewalk with him (perhaps we could revive those
they-must-step-off-the-sidewalks-when-one-of-our-women-
passes laws, not based on *color,* of course, but just on—well,
dirtiness, penury or something), and we must admit that
when the Republicans showed that released rapist's face on

television during the presidential campaign, *he* came to mind, and our wives and we shuddered. It's a shame, an awful, awful shame what's happened to him, but he had opportunities and he wasted them. It's no one's fault but his own, and we are installing new alarm systems in our homes, organizing neighborhood watches and talking to the city council and the zoning board about maybe putting up a gate on both ends of the block or the general area or something to let the politicians know because they're too afraid of the special interest groups to do anything about crime, and shouldn't we get those people off the streets anyway?

Or: there he is, returned home from college after four years, and he has grown so sure and so hostile that he cannot speak to us without glaring. We slap him on his back in greeting and he doesn't smile. We say that we are proud of him and he simply nods. No doubt this frosty unfriendliness is the work of black revolutionary Black Panther professors. They have filled his mind with rebellion, with I-hate-honkies nonsense, and yes, there has been racism in the past but violence doesn't solve anything. He lauds that madman Farrakhan and wishes to organize a local political group for Jesse Jackson (and yes, of course, it's good that a black man can run for president in this country nowadays—it couldn't even happen in another country—but that man is a loudmouth, we don't trust him, and he has no real political experience). We have even heard that he quit the football team. Behind his black eyes he plots the burning of cities. That he is articulate, that he wields an Ivy League degree (and our nephew didn't get into Princeton, imagine!), these facts simply make him more dangerous. We know he's plotting. And we know he wants a white woman, or a white *bitch,* which is what they call them, he wants to do horrible, horrible things to her, throw her down onto a dirty mattress without sheets in a putrid, cockroach-infested room and slobber his big purple lips all over her face making it rancid with his AIDS-carrying saliva (he does drugs, sells them, we knew it, from out of a BMW, probably) and mangle her poor breasts with huge, huge hands and fuck her, fuck her with his big, purple and black, 18-inch gorilla dick, thrashing, humping, pummeling into her as he slaps her until she begs him to stop, oh she's crying, she's crying, our poor, sweet daughter and the others are waiting, ugly big black ape men cheering him on and one sticks his into her mouth NIGGER! Yes, NIGGER! Nigger, nigger, nigger! We just want to stand up while he's speaking in the high school auditorium right now and scream his name NIGGER, except that's not strong enough they call themselves that, GORILLA! APE!! And grab his fucking neck and kick him and cut his bigblackthing off and fuck *him,* yes *fuck* him so he knows how it feels the big black—and that's what he needs, probably. He's so depraved he probably wants it.

Ah, but this is where we falter, because He cannot be penetrated. His orifices, if we can be naughty with our metaphors, are not open to us. We cannot know him. It is not that he lacks an inner life, only that his language—if it be language at all—is alien. We could not understand.

I, alone on my park bench, can do no better in the singular than in the collective. To me he is beautiful: cruelty in his mouth, sex (sex of the possessive type, no mutuality, only taking and devouring) in his broad shoulders and his narrow pelvis. Tenderness in his eyes and slender calves. He is intelligent—so his smirk tells me. I watch him with this woman and my whole body yearns simply to be one curled hair beneath his hanging testicles, or one bead of sweat rolling languorously down his chest to drip from the tip of his erect brown nipple. Oh, he is a black *man,* a man of African descent, and I fell for him ages ago. Every fact—about AIDS, homicide, drugs, violence, education, income, health, life expectancy—says differently, but I see him and know he is all right with the world. *Come to me, pupu,* as Cyrus would say, and add that fierce deep in the throat late-in-the-hot-afternoon-after-just-getting-it satiation sound Aretha makes when she sings "Dr. Feelgood." Oh yes, add that. His people, his community is *his; it is* a community. He gave up nothing he loved, embraced nothing he detested to become a part of it. He was its prince before he was born.

But see how deformed he is even in my looking, how driven to distraction with abstractions I am. Like the White Girls outside my apartment window, he defies me. I cannot inhabit him. A few guesses, maybe, here and there: in high school he dated white girls because they were bold enough to approach him; he was shy, and to be openly proclaimed the object of someone's desire, across racial lines even, was flattery to which he felt compelled to respond, lest it get away. Later he dated black women because they had become foreign to him over the years, exotic like spice islands in the Caribbean. He delighted in their "sassiness," which was the name he had learned to give to anything they said which expressed an opinion. In those locker rooms, those halls of worship, he too felt a part of himself aroused with guilty desire, but for one man only—his tall, tight jeans–wearing friend Frederick, his "boy." Sometimes on the bus after track meets they sat together, and Fred fell asleep on his shoulder. He would let him lay there, will his shoulder to become a cushion. He would study Fred's soft eyelashes, absorb Fred's smell in his clothes and his memory to carry home.

All such facts have to do with the presence or absence of women, of course. By the presence of women and how he relates to them (preferably as objects, toys, servants) and the absence of women and how he speaks of them ("We gon tear us up some pussy tonight, ain't we, Fred?"), his (my, your) manhood is established. We would perhaps learn a great deal about him if we knew that the women he is most drawn to, most obsessed with, are Marta and Elaine, two svelte-hipped lesbian lovers who transferred to his school from Yale (say he went to Howard, or else to Morehouse, and the dykes transferred to Spelman). In their presence he is not so much unmanned as simply jealous; he imagines that their lives, most particularly their sex lives, are far more exciting than his own. But this woman he walks with, he has her in hand. She is not with him willingly—for that would suppose she has will, and, young, she has not yet discovered that quality—but she was not precisely forced, either. She will serve the usual functions—he will assign her a role, indifferently, as one might choose to snack between meals—then he will discard her, but not without sympathy, so that she will not be able to blame him but will instead wonder what is wrong with herself. And because we delight to see him as we have created him, we do not warn but encourage her. Hang yourself on him, we urge. Leave the noose that fits his neck for our devising.

No, I cannot tell his story as he would tell it. It is, in part, my story, and the closer the two become, the less able I feel to narrate. He has so many faces. As an adolescent I pictured him and hoped to become him. At that time his skin color was high yellow rather than blue-black as now; he wore a white T-shirt, had (of course) a muscular chest, a mustache, curly "good" hair, and—get this—drove a white pickup. (I did grow up in Kansas City. . . .) Most important: all the girls adored him. (For a moment—a brief moment—he was my cousin Hammett, imbued as no other—until Evan, maybe—with the transformative power of sex.) He hasn't changed very much. His politics are better, certainly, but apart from cosmetics he is the same: what we wish for. And if we misapprehend him, if our looking destroys him, well—in this day and age, one can only love another by first loving his stereotype.

Today I inhabit him, it, them, and me.

Good-bye, Hammett.

I loved you.

25

THE ADVENTURES OF EVAN
MARCIALIS

Central Park is huge. It doesn't seem any smaller now than when I was a little kid, which is kind of strange. When I finally went back to Mom's grave everything looked like it had shrunk. The cemetery grounds and the trees. Mom's tombstone.

For eight years I didn't even see it, Mom's tombstone. Daddy stopped going when he got remarried, and he asked Nicholas and me if we wanted to go sometimes, but we said no. I said no because Nicky said no, and because Daddy seemed like he didn't want us to go. Just that way Daddy has of asking when he really isn't giving you a choice. But for my twentieth birthday I went back finally, and it was like a doll's graveyard compared to what I remembered.

I thought I might go there today, but I don't have time, and I need a bigger space, like here, which never

shrunk because I never stopped coming here. Here is where
Kenneth comes, every day almost, if I'm at work.

What does he do here all day? He's so mysterious
about it. He walks around or sits around and dreams up romantic stories for us, I guess, or comes up with scenes.

We haven't done a real Game in ages, unless I count
my scene, which I don't even want to think about now. And
then the other night, that weird sex, it was—weird. Like it
kind of was a Game, too, but I didn't know what part I was
playing—which should be no surprise, since sometimes it
seems like everybody wants to be some kind of Svengali in
my life. Like Allan this morning. He pushed me around the
set—he didn't touch me but he pushed—threw me up next
to Vicki every chance he got, and then sent that smiley *Soap
Opera Digest* woman over to us. Vicki did almost the same
thing yesterday, but more gracefully of course because of
who she is, but still. She like upped the ante on our friendship overnight and suddenly instead of giving each other
backrubs and light touches and hugging, it's lip smooches
and sitting on my lap and putting her head on my lap, almost between my legs. Which is fine, but. And Kenneth,
too, I'm always *his,* the sexually aggressive one if he wants
it, the cheerful one if he wants that, the one who plays the
bad guy in our scenes, whatever.

I guess—it's not bad, actually. It's really not bad at all.
Because everything they ask me to do or want me to do
without asking is okay. It's comfortable, kind of. Sometimes
it's great, like the scenes Ken and I do. I mean, the roles I
play are the roles everyone expects, and they're not so bad.
It's not like being expected to fill the role of a janitor or
anything. The roles I get in life and on the stage, those are
the parts everyone else wants to play. Like when Kenneth

and I both auditioned for the soap, and I get callbacks for the likable, young, horny but really good-hearted ingenue doctor's son, and Ken gets called back for a hospital orderly with two lines. So they're not bad roles.

But.

If Ken was here by himself and thinking about stuff like this, he'd *inhabit* something. Take a detail like that red dust from Egypt story Vicki told me, which he made into the airport story.

But me, I feel like I'm only good at thinking about things I've actually done, or somebody else did. Like about how we used to play Planet of the Apes here in the park. Me, Benjy, Mike, John, and Russ sometimes, and once my brother even played for about two seconds. I must've been around nine then, and the TV show *Planet of the Apes* was on, with the boring blond guy and the cute dark-haired guy and General Urko. Mike played General Urko most of the time. He walked bent over with his arms hanging and snorted his nostrils just like a gorilla. The way we played it, it was just Cowboys and Indians all over again, except the humans didn't have any weapons and always got chased. It was so much fun to be chased through the park and run through the wooded places and around ponds and down hills. I was kind of a troublemaker because we were supposed to switch to gorilla when we got caught, but I never wanted to. I insisted on being human. I didn't want to chase anyone; I didn't want to be the violent one. I didn't want to be strong the way Mike was strong. I cried and kicked and screamed, and even being called a crybaby wouldn't change my mind. Everyone would get mad and threaten to quit when I did it, but I got my way.

I don't know why I was so stubborn about it. I feel

like I can think of reasons now, but I don't know if they're right, if I'm just doing what we always do, making up some big long story that explains everything and connects every little random piece of your life. But the connection between *Planet of the Apes* and other things seems so clear to me. After a few years, when we'd stopped playing Apes and I was maybe twelve or something, it did matter to me whether or not I got called a crybaby, or a sissy or a fag, which basically everybody got called if they did anything anyone else thought was stupid. Guys got called fag ten times a day in my neighborhood. Sissy was much worse. That was for *real*. My life started to get real secretive about that time. I would be ashamed to think about how I acted when we played Apes, and if anybody teased me about it, I'd get mad and start punching. What was open for everyone to see when I was nine had to go underground. I didn't share my secrets with anyone except Philip. Phil was a serious comic book fan like I was, and we used to sit around and talk about Thor and the Sub-Mariner and the Avengers for hours. Everyone else read comics, too, but just for the action. They'd want to talk about how cool it was that Iron Man and Thor got in a fight, or who was stronger, Vision or Wonder Man. Phil and I were totally into the history, the characters' lives, the whole mythology of the Marvel Universe. We talked alone, in secret, and we didn't tell the other guys how into it we were that in the Avengers, Mantis, Vietnamese bargirl and martial arts mistress, turned out to be the Celestial Madonna, the earth woman who would mate with a sentient tree and one day give birth to the ruler of the heavens. We loved Mantis. She was tough, she went after the man she wanted no matter how anyone else felt, and she could beat Thor. We never said anything in public, but anyone who said that Mantis was a bitch, or said she was ugly, we hated. We'd take spells out of Dr. Strange, Master of the Mystic Arts comics, and cast them against people who didn't like Mantis. We drew pictures of her and hid them in a secret folder that Philip kept because he was an only child and my brother was nosy. Our biggest secret together was that we cried when she left planet Earth to live in the heavens with the tree guy.

It's sad to me that we felt like we had to be so secretive about the games we wanted to play.

In an acting class once the teacher told us to sit down on the floor and clear our minds, and sit there breathing slowly with our eyes closed until we found an image that made us feel calm and right. It was supposed to be a vision quest exercise, like the Plains Indians who would starve for days and then be visited by animal spirits like bears and eagles, and the spirits would bond with them. A few people came up with animals—some guy said a cobra, but he was lying. Why would a cobra represent anything really deep to anybody, really part of your essence, for people in urban and suburban America? Most of us who were serious came up with things from our own worlds. Some girl said Walter Cronkite came to her. For me it was Mantis. She looked a lot like my mom does in her pictures, at least around the eyes, which were kind of dark and Asiatic. Except Mom had blond hair and is supposed to've had real pale skin.

When I picture my mom I picture Mantis, and when I think of Mantis I think of my mom.

Now, what I'm supposed to get out of thinking about all that I don't know. . . .

But it is sad to me, how even when you decide to live

a life of play like I have, you have to kick and scream to
play it the way you want to play it, or you have to do it in
secret.

I guess I should get back to work.

26

SELVES AND VOICES

KENNETH WATCHES: The Park is vast, and sometimes I get lost in it. I had found a different spot, closer to the east side, and I slept in the shade on a bench until a child stormed by on her bicycle with noisy training wheels. She screamed pure joy and awakened me in time to see her mother jet by after her. Now, on my way back west, backpack full of unread magazines slung over one shoulder, I've come upon a thickly green and hilly area, full of damp and shadow.

I've never seen it before. Am I up higher than usual? In the 90th Street range? The weeds grow high here, and with the sagging branches of the trees they capture the park benches in verdant cages. The paths are unpaved and muddy with the recent rain, and they rise and fall into clumps of dark bushes.

And there are men here. One man stands there, another walks his dog there; still another passes by quietly, a ghost in sunglasses. Away to my left three men sit on a bench in the weeds; from their gestures and body movements they are laughing, I think, but the distance, and the green, swallow the sound. I see no women, only men. In the humidity they are like denizens of a jungle. And what emanates from them, like steam heat.

A man asks me the time. His voice, as carefully cut and blow-dried as his dyed pitch-black hair, startles me. His eyes, brown and jaded, advertise an invitation that his words no not speak. But I grumble the time—4:35 P.M.—and move on. As if I were really contemplating something anyway. Perhaps he sneers at my retreating back. Perhaps he places me at the center of some fantasy, and today and tonight and for months to come I shall be pulled out, like a card in a hidden Rolodex, and be made to swallow his testicles or present my naked ass for his discipline and ravishment.

The possibility appeals to me, but I am not at ease with its allure. I carry the imprint of his watchful, appraising eyes on my back and out from beneath the trees, away from the jungle and onto the street. The feel of his eyes makes me tense. When Evan settles his blue eyes upon my body, when he takes time, as he sometimes does, to hold his chin in thumb and forefinger and hold me in his view, I squirm and bridle. I shield myself with race-curses that flow easily from me like the verses of a long-practiced incantation—how dare you objectify me in this way, how can you make me a slab of meat like a slave at an auction: these are what I think to say, while refusing to meet his gaze. But the spell catches in my throat. It fails to name what it seeks to control. It is not precisely a racial body that I do not wish him to see, but more idiosyncratic selves: shamed family selves, ignorantly happy childhood selves, selves that fear love and fear sex and crave both with an unheeding rapaciousness. Selves that climb trees and hide when my brothers scour the neighborhood recruiting for a pickup basketball game, that lip-synch Diana Ross in the mirror before Dad gets home. Selves that need to be protected, that cannot bear to behold their own reflections in Evan's eye like a thousand images in the hideous compound orbs of a fly.

Yes, a fly—my selves multiply like flies. Walking down the street now, no one suspects that I am a swarm, a buzzing, twitching, colony creature. I come stalking souls, I want to warn them, though the warning would avail them nothing, for still I come, relentless. I come to meld your soul into mine, my memories into yours. I come crossing boundaries, hurdling over barriers. I come, and when I am through we shall scarcely be able to tell the one from the other: we shall be fragments, shards, as of a shattered mirror, never whole and fully functioning unless together, but sharp and brilliant when apart.

It is true that I'd rather not be seen as you would see me—you, the throng passing on the street in navy blue suits and casual summer dresses. Your seeing threatens me. In your sight I become undone. But I will bear your seeing me. I shall wear the imprint of your eyes on my back. For if in seeing me you only recreate that which is some part of you, then the tunnel of vision is open on both ends. Even as you see me I collect and acquire your vision for my own purposes. Gathering you up, I learn to speak in the many voices you insist are not my own.

Ah, *voices,* you say, *from sight to sound without a beat. He speaks his insanity, he mixes his metaphors, because he hears voices.*

And, yes, I do hear voices. I speak them—tongues, if you will. But when I hear them I do not amble out unshaven on moonless nights wielding an ax with which to cleave coeds into bloody halves, nor run about giggling and chirping to the flowers as I toss back my long hair and clutch at my dress while white-coated men whisper *hush* and usher me into the back of an ambulance. My voices speak to me as some other, yes, but in the first person, too, like a memory, like someone I once knew, loved and have forgotten. Like me, a mysterious collective "I," cast loose from its moorings ages ago, which now returns, bobbing slowly up and down like a buoy in the flowing and receding tide.

So I cross the street against the traffic. I ignore the fury of the car horns, the shouts, the looks of horror. I am nimble. I am quick. I am (Cyrus speaks now) the Bomb.

Today I am inhabited.

27

A CONVERSATION IN TWO TALES

They sit together. Kenneth is on the floor between Evan's spread legs, with his back to Evan's stomach. Evan, practicing skills bequeathed him by Kenneth's mother during her last visit, is oiling Kenneth's scalp. Usually during this ritual they gossip, but tonight the blank silence tells both of them that it is time to talk.

KENNETH WATCHES: If only it could all end here and now. I like endings. They satisfy.

If I had my way I'd decree an ending. An exotic locale would be necessary—perhaps a littered alleyway in Bangkok, wet with rain and soiled with discarded condoms and scraps of unclaimed clothing. But that lacks epic sweep, and an ending is not an ending without epic sweep.

An exotic locale: a Mediterranean port city's harbor, at sunset. For this to work, the sky should have the color of a blood orange, or of a dying rose. A woman is standing at the rail of a ferry boat. The boat moves slowly out to sea and trails a thin blue V over the surface of the calm water. We see the woman's face: it is composed and wistful, melancholy and resolute. We see her face, but it is her point of view we are meant to share. In her face, and in us as we see and inhabit her face, there is a sadness, a sense of loss, immeasurable loss, and the herculean strength to accept and bear its incalculability. She wears a light trenchcoat, gray, or blue; it is unnecessary in the humidity, but she wears it because she must have something to brace herself against her loss. A small suitcase (it matches the coat) sits forlornly at her feet.

On the pier she and we see two men—young men, beautiful. One dark, one light. They wear ratty pullover sweaters, droopy khaki shorts, and construction worker boots. They have very fine legs. We feel the boundlessness, the insatiable ache, of our need for them. Their faces are composed and cool, unhurried and peerlessly lovely.

One turns his head, but without apparent urgency or intent, almost distractedly. We and she see his profile—a Semitic or African or Roman nose, perhaps, full lips, locks of wine-dark hair lank across his forehead or thick upon his head. The other notices—barely—that the first has turned, and now his face turns, too. This other's eyes are green, or blue, or an accidental shade of brown that has no other purpose than to be marveled at. Their noses almost touch, their lips just brush. We hear them sigh, and one's hand moves with lackadaisical ardor over the other's chest. His hand rests there.

We pull away now. The two beauties become two figures among many others, of far less beauty, which stand on the dwindling pier. Ramshackle homes with ceramic tile roofs rise above the men's splendid heads, and then evergreen hills and red stone villas, and then the sky, infinite—a blood orange, a fading rose on the day before it dies.

It is over. The mystery is solved. The body, or the object of value or power, has been found. Everyone knows who everyone is. The lovers are happy, and they're not coming back.

. . . Kind of my ideal Hardy Boys episode or novel ending. Of course, substitutions in casting are always possible, and encouraged. I would never cast Parker Stevenson or that embarrassment, Shaun Cassidy, for example. Frank could be an exquisitely dark Afro-Brazilian guy, Joe a blondish Greek-American, the woman a man, maybe a redhead, from Orange County in southern California. Or me, Evanitch, and somebody I don't like much but would love to have, like Tom Cruise. Maybe—just a thought, I don't know if it works at all—maybe's he's Hammett.

This city might be Alexandria or Venice, Tangier or Athens, Rome or Tel Aviv. In each, hidden at the end of an obscure alley, lies the white stucco facade of a modest home, behind which Lord Cyrus lounges poolside on an enormous patio of marble tiles, pearly columns, and topaz fountains. He is attended by an army of well-endowed, silent men whose heads are cleanly shaven.

The best thing about an ending like that is that I can forget for a moment what I know:

That there is no real purity, no true innocence, and no escape in desire or love or fantasy.

Oh, and one more perk, too, one more compensatory pleasure to be snatched from the stingy hands of the gods: I never feel, being part of a scene, what I feel watching it.

There is greater depth in participation, of course, more passion, but never the sheer immensity of spectatorhood, the uncanny sensation of space and emotion expanding around me as my senses grow large, godlike, to reach over blocks, whole cities, across oceans, no longer confined to a single act of love, a single page of a single book. Only by watching can I live a myth, or breathe a symbol, or make love to the untainted, ecstatic glory of a *type*.

But of course that brings me right back to what I'm trying to forget.

Tonight, I inhabit a face, a casual caress, and an immeasurable, immeasurable loss.

THE ADVENTURES OF EVAN MARCIALIS: Daddy didn't take us much to church after Mom died, so I never got that thing that other people get, where if your life really falls apart or something traumatic happens, you can always go back to the church. Sometimes that feels like an option I'd want to have.

I want to tell Kenneth something, a story, which is what made me think of church. What I used to like about church were the parables, those stories Jesus and the prophets told. They were supposed to be real simple, with easy quick lessons for dumb slow unbelievers, but they really weren't that simple. It always turned out that they were a way to show that everything that's supposed to be simple is actually totally complicated.

So all week long I've had this kind of parable brewing in my head, and I'm thinking that maybe this would be a way to say something important, if I can just get it out right.

"There was this Puerto Rican guy. Ramon Ayala-Vasquez. I'd say his name out loud at night. I'd whisper it at my window: *Rrraw-moann I-jawla Bvas-keezz.* I hoped that if I said it just right I'd see him. I hoped he'd float to the other side of the windowpane.

"You'd like this: Ramon had black, tough-boy hair and black, tough-boy eyebrows and cruel, rich lips. He had black, little-boy eyelashes. And brown skin, like shoe leather. If he really ever did come to the window, I'd've been scared.

"They said Ramon hated white people. He never talked to any, never smiled at any, never would be nice to anyone white. This was just known. It was not a fact anyone I knew ever questioned. You might be like me and say you didn't blame him, or you might say he was why you were afraid of Puerto Ricans, but one thing you knew was that he hated white people. The reason this made any difference at all to the people who talked about it in my freshman dorm was that Ramon was hot. He could make, like, the straightest, nastiest, fag-bashing Italian football player salivate.

"Now, it wasn't exactly clear that Ramon was gay. But one of the first things I learned from my giggly queerboy friends was that if you looked at Ramon the right way, if you said the right thing at the right time—if you like begged, and didn't get too loud about it—and then if you were white and pretty like me and my friends, and not rich, too—if you were cute white *trash*—then Ramon would go back to wherever you wanted to go and fuck the shit out of you.

"You didn't get to touch him. Anywhere. Ever. He didn't want to talk, except to tell you to strip, bend over, lie back, shut up, or get the fuck away. But he fucked you good. *Really* good. For hours. He'd come a couple of times, but he wouldn't help you come. And even if you came and wanted to stop, he wouldn't pull out until he was ready. And then you, like everybody he ever did it to, would call him for some more. And he might—he'd let you beg for a while, maybe a long time if he really thought you were pretty—then he might fuck you one last time. And he'd fuck the *shit* out of you. He'd roll his ass around and plug your ass like this piston prod trying to get everywhere in-side you, like he was trying to hit every inch of you inside. He was lean, and his dick was really big and had this really big round head. Not that he'd let you see it. He'd only fuck you with it. You got to know its shape by the feel of it up your ass.

"He fucked you *good.*

"And they say he came like heaven.

"Now, I never did it with him. I wanted to. But I would kind of just keep an eye on him. If I saw him, I'd hover. I kept trying to figure out what it was I should say to him and how I should say it. But I could never figure out the way to do it. One time I was so disgusted with myself for not saying anything that I decided to follow him—he'd already passed by, kind of glanced; I didn't say anything as usual and he kept walking. I followed him. And then he stopped and waited for a while, on a corner. I thought he was waiting for me and I got scared, so I stopped, too, and looked around at a store window or something. Finally I came to the decision that it was now or never, and so I turned around.

"A short, stocky black guy was there. He and Ramon hugged each other tight and kissed. The black guy kind of patted Ramon's ass, and then they kissed again. Then they walked right past me, talking. Ramon didn't even glance at me.

"I still jack off thinking about Ramon. He's always hot when I think of him, always mean but really *good,* and he never takes his pants all the way off. He's always fucking, and he slaps the guy's ass with his hand, and with his lean, mean brown hips. The guy he fucks is always white, with long blond hair and blue eyes, but he doesn't really have a face. I blot him out, in a way. I only think about Ramon and his pleasure. Ramon grunts and pumps and talks dirty and abusively until I come. The white guy loves it.

"Now, before Ramon I never thought much about all that top and bottom stuff. Some guys, a lot of guys, worry about who fucks and who gets fucked, who fucked who first, who likes getting fucked more than fucking. After Ramon, I really started to get into all that, in a way. Just to think about it. And to be honest, I can't separate thinking about that stuff from thinking about Ramon and his fucking—and it always gets me excited."

Now Kenneth speaks:
"I felt like I had betrayed Hammett. By sleeping with you. By sleeping with a white man. That's what almost everything since he died's been about for me. And maybe there is some betrayal there. But not in *loving* you and sleeping with you. Or even if it was just sleeping with you, just lust, that's not the betrayal. The real betrayal, of him and of you, was believing that he was powerless, that he was this Charlie-Brown-in-blackface nobody reaching for some little piece of glory he'd never find. And that in order to embrace him I had to embrace *that.* And thinking you were

that's opposite: power. And feeling like I had to embrace the kind of power I thought you were in order to embrace you. Which is true, in a way, but never necessarily true. You know what I mean? The other night, that was as close as I could get to following through with those two feelings. But it didn't work, because neither view has to be. Either or both *could* be true, but they didn't have to be. Neither conception could ever tell me who or what either of you were or are, not completely. They could only tell me what some of your roles were.

"Do you understand?"

Evan answers. "Yeah. Yeah. I think I totally understand that."

28

EVAN AND KENNETH

Each touched the other's nipples with wet fingers. Both tin
gled. Kenneth made much of the producer-prescribed iron
ripples of Evan's stomach, and both of them became very
excited by Kenneth's excitement. They made out like high
school boys, sloppily and with lots of tongue.

"I love you," Evan says.   "I'm sorry," Kenneth says.
"I love *you*," Kenneth says.   "I'm sorry, too," Evan says.

Having told truths and lies, they now sleep comfort-
ably, side by side, with their arms folded across their chests
like dead Egyptian kings.

29

A PLAY READING, AND DISCUSSION AFTERWARDS

PLAYERS: KENNETH GABRIEL AS HIM
CYRUS LOCKE AS HE

The Script:

Darkness.

The tide can be heard.

At length it becomes possible to discern two shapes in the darkness, black silhouettes against the gray.

A small spotlight shines suddenly upon the figure stage right. His face can be seen, almost yellow in the illumination. A large, floor-to-ceiling, wall-to-wall movie screen flares into life behind both figures. In grainy black-and-white it reflects onscreen what the spotlight shows: his blue-with-golden-stripes Egyptian headdress, the coiled cobra uraeus serpent on his brow; his face, regal and handsome; his neck and shoulders decorated with broad, close-set rings of gold jewelry; his arms and hands, rings with fat stones on each finger; his waist, encircled by a thick brown gold-studded leather belt; his short blue-trimmed-with-gold skirt, its ends cut in a broad, flat-bottomed V that divides his legs; and finally his feet, sandaled.

The spotlight moves to the figure stage left. The screen again shows what the spotlight shows, but the pictures are bright, clear slides, changing in rapid fire like photographs taken at a model shoot. It starts with his feet, which are calloused and ugly. Then other, isolated parts of his body are seen: a muscled calf, turned at some classic angle, quadriceps, hamstring muscles, hip, abdomen, hands, chest, shoulders, biceps, neck—all naked and quite beautiful. The genitals are last, and are enormous. (Perhaps a fast drumbeat as these pictures flash across the screen.)

Darkness again, the sound of the sea suddenly loud now as the surf breaks. Then quiet, and larger, full-body light on figure stage right, who remains motionless.

HE: I looked for him, by declaring that his features were merely of a mass, indistinguishable from others of his ilk. I loved him, by declaring him worthy of no better than indifference, no worse than incidental contempt. I chased him, by ostentatiously refusing to even nod in his direction. So it was. This is our story, as I shall call it, though "our" lacks its usual collective possessive denotation here.

Some officer sent him to fetch me one night, when I stood alone on the quiet shore of the Red Sea. Some officer spoke the command, but it was a god who sent him. This I know because if my thoughts and worries that evening could have been clothed in flesh, they would come to me as he did. There is, you see, a stench which clings to men of power, like a sweat of garlic on the skin. I had grown to detest that stench. I had grown to detest the hard face I must show to my enemies, those of Egypt and not of Egypt; I had grown to detest my own cruelty, my own hard hunger that crushed competitors, that mercilessly killed with a broadsword and scarred with a whip. I had grown to detest the cost of empire—the cost to me. What would it be, I wondered, to be soft? To bend, to surrender, to give, to wait? To wait in the service of another man.

So he came to me, and when I saw him I knew that his was the sweet body I needed, that in his slattern's gait was a defiance and will to power I could mold as my own. I bought him that very night. And, with careful instruction and honeyed reassurances, I took him to my abode and had my way with him having his way with me.

Another light on figure stage left. HE *can still be seen, but the figure's face on stage remains outside the spotlight. This figure shifts his position from time to time, in relaxed, graceful movements.*

HIM: He was *fine.* That smooth aristocratic soldier look, big daddy shoulders and big ol' arms, that deep brown-black color. He was something I've always

wanted, but could never have. Now I know I'm not
supposed to say that, being supposedly a slave and all,
and being supposedly a man and all who wants ven-
geance on his captors. I want revenge, all right, but I
was never much for the arts of war, which is why Miss
Mama kept me in the house when the Egyptians came
in talking battle in Megiddo and drafting all able
young men into the service. But when those bitches
busted up into the house like they were going to kill
somebody, you mark me, I fought like a hellcat. They
didn't know what hit them. They got me down and
beat my ass, and to punish me they made me a slave,
but, hey, I took some of their eyeballs with me into
slavery.

Later on I calmed down. Because however much they
wanted to punish me, being owned by the Egyptian
army isn't exactly the worst thing a boy like me could
be. Miss Mama always said that I was gifted with an
excess of desire.

So then when he said, you are mine now, and I want
you to do this to me, and that and this—hey. I said,
watch me.

HE: Tonight I will belong to him. I will be a criminal,
accused of a heinous crime against the gods, thrown to
my hands and knees before his feet. I will kiss his bare
feet, and cry for mercy I will not receive. I will be
judged and sentenced. I will be beaten slowly by his
bare hands. Taken with brutality. I will be made to

serve his desires and given no pleasure, no pleasure at all.

HIM: What he said. Myself, I just want to be sure I don't leave any bruises on his skin. Inside—well that's different.

(HIM *provocatively touches himself, as we finally see his face.*)

Now, I myself adore fantasies. I recommend them. Sometimes you just have to be careful, that's all.

"When I read this before, I really hadn't thought about playing HIM," Kenneth says apologetically. He is ashamed of his performance.

"But you do it so well." This is not the tone of voice that will set Kenneth at ease. Cyrus is in director mode and very, very cool.

Kenneth, breathing now, leaves the small stage to sit in the row in front of Cyrus. His mind is not at all on his words when he says, "Who would play HE—I mean, if I, supposing I got cast?"

"Mmmm. Well, Douglas will want to play HE, I think, since he wrote it. He's a fool, if you ask me, but I'm not sole artistic director and Helen wants him. He does have an instinct for the dramatic gesture, I'll admit, and he's popular, so he'll bring people in. With a little tinkering, this play could have a decent run and probably turn a profit if we put together some nice posters with hot half-naked men in *Ten Commandments* costumes on it—and if we don't go to the expense of doing the video portions in exactly the way Douglas wants it done. It's in ancient Egypt,

so it's got a bit of that Afrocentric thang; its two main characters are black homosexuals, so it's got that black-men-
loving-black-men thang; it has disturbing S/M imagery, so
it's got that shock thang; and then the things the characters
say and do sort of deconstructs all those categories, so it's
got that subversive thang, too." He shrugs and turns the
palms of his hands to the sky, his first gesture of the evening. "What more could an avant-garde African-American
not-sole artistic director of a struggling avant-garde African-
American theater in search of something slightly commer-
cial but not too compromising want?"

Kenneth laughs, which makes Cyrus smile and relax,
too. The theater seems unreasonably dark to him, and cold;
Cyrus's pleasure is something he can warm himself with.
"Odd . . . the parallels, I mean. The fantasy material of the
play. The sex games. It's a minor part of the plot, but . . ."

"That's why I had you read that scene." He still hasn't
said what he thinks of Kenneth's audition.

"You didn't mention what Evan and I do to Douglas,
did you?" It seems a silly question, but it sets Kenneth up
for just what he wants, which is what Cyrus gives him:

"Sweetheart, *everybody* is ready for what you and Big
Blond *do* because everybody does it. Some folks, Douglas in-
cluded, are just not ready for the fact that you two—or
what they think you two are—do it. But *games.*" Cyrus
sighs with theatrical world-weariness.

(KENNETH WATCHES: Why is Cyrus the one in the
audience, while I'm—maybe—the one on stage?)

"Games everybody plays. I didn't need to tell Douglas
anything. Now Luther, child, my hot hot no-account man,

has started a new game, the old game called caricature. *You* like the sunrise; I, the sunset, he tells me. I can't live if I don't BLANK; you would die if you did. That sort of thing: creating opposition for its own sake. Each morning with the ham and eggs we get a rundown of what I'm like that he isn't. The better to serve his private sense of tragedy, his fantasy of innocence. I overwhelm him, you see, and this is how he handles it. And I just say *mmm-hm*, because the boy has something, whether it's between his legs or whatever, that I have to have. Neither you nor Douglas has to teach me about games."

He begins to rise from his chair. "Has Daria or anybody said anything to you about the Hammett case? Have the police found anything?"

Kenneth shakes his head. "Someone apparently said that they remember seeing a skinny blond guy in a car with a bunch of guys. Very vague. The police think it's not much to go on. I don't think it is, either."

"And how do you feel about that?"

"Numb. Furious," Kenneth answers.

Cyrus tilts his head toward Kenneth and gives him an over-the-rims-of-his-glasses-hard-life-lessons look. "I understand that. And those feelings may never stop, Kenneth. They'll fade, but they won't stop. That's how it is, with injustice. You just—struggle on."

"Mm," Kenneth agrees. "You won't be going to the dance-riot demonstration, will you? It's tomorrow."

Cyrus's lips twist. "I'll be otherwise occupied," he says. Then he smiles. "But—have a good time."

He is through the doorway, with Kenneth following slowly behind, before he brings his hand to his mouth in mock horror and says, "Oh! I forgot. You've got the part."

30

DANCE, MUSIC, SEX, RIOT

This was how it happened:

At 7:39 A.M., Shanika Lopez's head of rust-colored hair and high yellow face appeared at sidewalk level, followed by her wide hipped body wrapped up tight in a dress of bright, insouciant patterns. She shook the subway station off of her and felt very bitter. She loved a pithy line, and one of her top twenty was "I do not approve of morning."

So today she frowned fiercely at the men who stared at her and tucked closer to her size-34 bosom her two nine-pound art books: Popova and Malevich, stolen two years ago from the University of California at Berkeley art library, and now, sadly, to be sacrifices to the cause.

Shanika was walking in low heels that morning, so that the pasty, obese fellow in the blue police shirt sitting heavily on his scooter just below and beside the curb seemed even shorter to her than he might otherwise have (she was 5′ 10″ and would have modeled if she were a different complexion and a bit slimmer). She felt even more bitter seeing him, because he was at that moment writing down a car's license plate number to give the driver a ticket. She stopped and glared at him. The policeman saw her, and glared—well, leered and glared—back at her. She checked her watch. Then, raising the intensity of her original glare as best she could, she hoisted the two excruciatingly weighty books into either hand above her head, and cried, "If thou wilt not live by Art, then *die* by Art!" And hurled the books right at fat boy's head.

(It was possible, though not probable, that the policeman exploded when the books hit him. Shanika couldn't see in the ensuing melee, but later she did manage to retrieve Popova, and the policeman was nowhere to be found.)

At 7:45 and 20 seconds A.M. a huge crowd—estimates ranged from fifteen hundred to nearly three thousand, depending on the newspaper—appeared in the very center of the financial district. They poured out of vans and cars and subway stations and hotel lobbies—mostly men, but women, too, young and middle-aged, men of color and white boys, some beautiful, others not, many wearing skirts over hairy legs and dangling huge hoop rings from their ears, all bursting onto the streets amid the morning traffic in a horde, on cue. Cars and taxis swerved into sidewalk curbs to avoid them; bleating horns and shouted obscenities resounded against the glass of the tall buildings.

The crowd charged howling, leaping onto car hoods, grabbing men wearing dour business suits off the sidewalk and twirling them around, disco-style, on the street. A hefty woman with a drum strapped to her chest pounded out a beat to a chant, which rose above the morning clamor: "DOWN!

DOWN! DOWN WITH THE PIGNAZIREPUBLICANS!"
they cried. And somewhere: "OFF WITH HIS HEAD!"

Before the police could arrive and clear them out, Evan
stood wiping off the sweat that wormed its way down from
his hairline and over his face. He wiped his eyes with the
arm of his sweater and looked about him with rising fear,
forcing his panicked gaze to rest on one figure, one face,
and then the next.

Kenneth was nowhere.

One wave of insanity after another jostled him. Ten or
more bearded black men swayed and stomped toward him
wearing fezzes and Nehru jackets, their choreographed steps
a mime of a New Orleans funeral march; they did not
chant, but periodically stopped and pointed in menacing
unison at some hapless onlooker and hissed, "SSSSSS-YYA!"
A tall stork-legged fellow in ancient Egyptian garb strode
behind them; he held aloft in his hands a boom box blast-
ing Mahalia Jackson's "Silent Night," which he used as a
weapon of terror, as when he scooped a fleeing businessman's head into his massive hand and held it against the
speakers. Did a white woman with big hair come rushing
up behind to jeer at the businessman? Were five guys with
Roman haircuts and pointed ears up there screaming, "Plak
tow!"? Evan was distracted by a dark brown older woman in
a red wig and a dress of green and violet veils; she bumped
into him and walked serenely on, her wrists and fingers en-
gaged in a symphony of grand gestures. A troop of yodeling
white boys, naked in blue paint traced in intricate whorls
on their bellies and necks and down the length of their
thighs, raced past. Their genitals, the only unpainted flesh
on their bodies, bounced around as if trying to get a better
look. Then away in the distance, above a vast plain of heads,

Evan glimpsed another naked figure, a black man with long sand-colored dreadlocks, straddling something that looked like the stone figure of a horse. The man's slender torso whipped back and forth in rhythmic abandon and his hair writhed about his shoulders as if he were a Gorgon. Like everyone else the man shouted, and waved a cat-o'-nine-tails in the air. "Mother wants her children to dance again! Mother wants her children to dance again!"

The gray morning air seemed flushed with the rosy glow of sunset. New York was blushing.

Evan stood, transfixed. Then he noticed that a couple of the rioters, big muscle types in black leather jackets and mean-looking boots, had stopped and were looking at him. Their heads inclined to one another as they whispered something. He saw their mouths shape the words, *Garth Gaines.*

Soap opera queens.

Not today, Evan thought. Not today, and maybe never again. "Kenneth!" Evan screamed, and began to run.

"There's a cure for AIDS!" shouted a jubilant woman and man, suddenly running beside him. On their respective foreheads were plastered the words (names?) PUSSY GALORE and COCK ABUNDANT. "Haven't you heard?! There's a cure!!" Some others took up the chant before it drowned in the general cacophony. For a moment Evan believed, began leaping, clenched fists in the sky. But just as suddenly he saw the feral scowl upon the couple's faces, and he understood.

Howling, leaping in fury now, Evan surged into the crowd. He tore off his shirt and tied it over his head like a pirate's bandanna. Everywhere about him was a whirl of color, flesh, and music, hideous faces of fear and wrath and exultation, and police sirens, rising and churning like a tornado funnel somewhere—somewhere on the edge, out there.

In the huge glass doors of one of the besieged buildings somewhere down the street, Kenneth thought he spied his reflection amid a wild pack of screaming men.

Later, in a sweaty jail cell packed with sweaty men, he remembered the reflection and having seen a face ablaze with such rapture that he could no longer be certain it had been his own.

POSTSCRIPT: MORE ABOUT HAMMETT

Flies, selves, tribbles and orcs are not alone: mysteries, too, have a way of multiplying.

For example, the mystery of why Addison Gabriel, Kenneth's uncle, hates so much. Some members of the family claim that the vessels of his body run with a scalding green liquid more bitter than bile and more vicious. In another world, another city, Addison could perhaps have been happy. He could have painted himself in garish whiteface and indulged his gleeful taste for torture and humiliation under a flashy sobriquet like The Joker, with only Batman and runny makeup to trouble him. With such an outlet, his home life might have been more pleasant. As this option was not available, Addison's wife Raye stood in for the helpless victims he could not tie to railroad tracks or hoist over vats of boiling oil.

The mystery of why Raye stood for this abuse with such passivity is another conundrum. She was a quiet, probably strong woman, certainly far from helpless in matters of the spirit, for she had come, over the years, to perceive clearly and without doubt the presence of a God at her shoulder who was not interested in judgment but concerned only with her personal welfare. "Nothin fazes Raye," other folks in her church said, and Raye nodded, *Ain't that the truth.*

One winter's morning a few months after Hammett's death, Raye said to Addison, "I don't believe we did that child right." Addison's response—a torrent of angry *bitchalwaysgotsomeshittosayfuckyofaggotdicksuckinsonIsmackyouupsideyosnatchbackhead;* an irrelevant arm-sweeping destruction of the arrangement of crystal unicorns set on Raye's side table; and a coat shoved in her face with *getthefuckoutmahhouse*—did not harm or faze Raye. "We did not treat him right," she repeated to the slammed back door of the house, and walked carefully over the ice in the driveway.

She took the car (luckily Addison didn't storm out with some mess about how she had no right to steal a man's car) and she drove to the cemetery. To apologize. The mystery of why this sentiment and resolution had not occurred to her before is yet another unsolved question. Raye had been to the grave of her only son (the issue of a short and unfortunate marriage, the less said the better) only once, at his funeral. She had covered her face and cried a great deal, but she had not thought to offer apologies. Her brother-in-law's wife, Parrie, had held her hand through the burial, and it was to Parrie's hand that she delivered the white business envelope with HAMMETT WADE written on it that she found in a fragile lean against the tombstone, at the end of a trail of prints in the snow made by somebody with big feet.

Raye and Parrie opened the envelope in the kitchen while the men were watching college bowl games, and they read the note together. It was typewritten and unsigned. Raye cried some more when they had finished and apologized again in her heart. Parrie didn't cry; she sent the letter on to Kenneth in New York. Kenneth read it, puzzled, cried a little himself, read it to Daria, then to Evan and Cyrus, and then gave it to the police. The police identified the typewriter which had produced the letter as being standard secretarial issue in several dozen workplaces, including NYPD precinct stations.

A copy remains in the WADE, H. homicide file; the original was returned to Raye, who gave it to Parrie for safekeeping.

The letter reads as follows:

I decided I better write this down, because if it is just in my head you might never know. I don't know exactly how this works, but that Spanish psychic woman you used to go to told me to do it this way.

This is for you, Ham. I'm too ashamed to speak it out loud anyway. And shame is what it's about, so why should I stop now? I can't stop. Shame is what let what happened to you happen. And envy.

I started out making up stories, in my mind. You found some chocolate man with muscles who treated you right, not like those white boys, one who treated you tenderly like you said you wanted. You ran past that alley and over a few blocks and you started walking, figuring I'd catch up with you, and you found him.

You went back to his place and he touched you, and in the morning he cooked sausage and eggs and smiled across the table. Then he touched you again, and you touched him. He was a man. A real man. I decided this was why I didn't hear from you the next day and the day after, and the day after.

Did you hear me laughing after I stopped running? I hope you didn't, brother, but it's been tearing me up to think you did. Because I was not laughing at you. I would never, and never did laugh at you, my own brother beyond blood. I laughed because it felt good to run. It sounds stupid, right? But it felt good to just run crazy. And it felt good to be with you, Ham, running crazy with you. I thought I was running with you.

I did not want to go back there for that woman who screamed. I knew it was a white woman. I kept laughing, and it felt so good. When I looked for you and did not find you, I decided you had hooked up. Later I decided that. I decided that later, when you didn't call me. I didn't call you either.

I guess that night I was probably afraid. I can write that. I swear to God Ham, I did not know what happened. I do not know now exactly what I thought. I had to get back, like I remember I told you earlier. Lois was coming back home and I didn't want her to know I was out with you. You know how she got about me going out with you. So I waited for a while, and then I left.

You were with a man. You been that way before, left me alone to go home with them. You made me mad like that before.

I want you to understand that. I did not know what happened, until that white woman's scream started to play over in my mind and started to sound like you screaming.

I hope you can understand why when I called the precinct over there I was anonymous.

I need you to forgive me, brother. Nobody could be boys like you and me could. I can write what I didn't say—I hope you have all the men you ever want up there where I know you are.

I love you, man. Please forgive me.

P.S. I saw your cousin. He didn't remember me at all. I hate him. I know you thought of him as close. But he betrayed you. He put your name out in the streets. He put what you were out there so everybody could see.

A NOTE ON THE TYPE

The typeface used in this book is one of many versions of Garamond, a modern homage to—rather than, strictly speaking, a revival of—the celebrated fonts of Claude Garamond (c. 1480–1561), the first founder to produce type on a large scale. Garamond's type was inspired by Francesco Griffo's *De Ætna* type (cut in the 1490s for Venetian printer Aldus Manutius and revived in the 1920s as Bembo), but its letter forms were cleaner and the fit between pieces of type improved. It therefore gave text a more harmonious overall appearance than its predecessors had, becoming the basis of all romans created on the Continent for the next two hundred years; it was itself still in use through the eighteenth century. Besides the many "Garamonds" in use today, other typefaces derived from his fonts are Granjon and Sabon (despite their being named after other printers).